We got to the bar where the band was playing at about nine. My nipples were clearly visible through my blouse and my cleavage was obvious. I noticed that a lot of men were stealing glances at me, including a guy whom Bill introduced as his friend Jack. And when Jack asked me to dance Bill said, 'Go ahead – you'll have a great time.'

He was right. Jack was a great dancer and when he held me close I could feel his cock getting hard. As the next song started, Jack kept me on the floor to dance again. This was a fast song and as I danced my skirt flared up. I realised that not only were the tops of my stockings showing, but anyone near the dance floor was getting a good view of my tiny black panties. I didn't feel ashamed at all, I just felt horny as hell . . .

Wild Abandon

Anonymous

HEADLINE

First published in Great Britain in 1992
by HEADLINE BOOK PUBLISHING PLC

10 9 8 7 6 5 4 3 2 1

ISBN 0 7472 3908 8

Printed and bound in Great Britain by
HarperCollins Manufacturing, Glasgow

HEADLINE BOOK PUBLISHING PLC
Headline House
79 Great Titchfield Street
London W1P 7FN

Wild Abandon

CHAPTER 1
Off to School

Hi! My name is Sharon. I grew up in a small town in upstate New York. In case you don't know, upstate New York has absolutely nothing in common with downstate, especially New York City. In 1969 I turned eighteen and I left for school in New York City. My life would never be the same again. Although I had a steady boyfriend, I was still a virgin. This was a condition that was not to last for long. This book is a chronicle of my time in the city.

I went to a two-year school that trained people to work in one of the businesses centered in New York. I ended up getting an education that far exceeded the promises of the college catalogue. Part of it was from school, but most of it was from the "secret" life I led there for so long. It started a little over a month after I got to school.

My roommate, Cindy, was three years older than I, but seemed at least ten. She had been all over the country and done all kinds of things. She told me that if I wanted to be a quick success in New York, I should learn to "fuck like a bunny." I told her that I had no intention of doing any such thing, but as time went on I began to change my mind.

I noticed that the few girls at school who were remaining loyal to boyfriends back home never went out at night or on weekends, and they were generally miserable; while the majority of girls assumed their boyfriends were sleeping with every girl they could, so they gladly accepted dates with eligible boys. Eligible boys meant anyone over the age of 18 and under 50 who could afford to take them out to dinner. The food at the school was really bad, so the girls always insisted that a date include dinner. They all seemed to think it was natural to spend the night with a boy if he spent enough money on you. I decided to quit being loyal, but I also decided that Bill (my boyfriend) should be the first to have me. He had been very patient all the time we had gone together.

CHAPTER 2
A Virgin No More

I caught a plane to Bill's college the second week of October. My roommate had made sure I got birth control pills the week before, but I was still scared when I got off the plane. I was lucky. We went out that night and I got just tipsy enough to be real hot after we left the bar. Bill looked so handsome that I just gaped at him, when he wasn't looking at me. He has kind of pale skin, but he tans real nice, so he looked dark after the summer. His hair is brown like mine, but the sun seems to bleach his out so he looks blond most of the time. And it's so fine, so incredibly fine. He never bothered to try to grow a beard or moustache, because he said his hair was so fine they didn't show up well. He also has green eyes that seem to set him apart from almost every other man that I know. They seem to sparkle when he looks at me. I suppose they do that for everyone, but I like to think it's because he loves me. At least that's what he tells me. I think he's just beautiful.

To get back to my story: I played with his cock all the way back to his apartment. I still can't believe he didn't have an accident driving his car, but we got there in about ten minutes. Bill had my skirt and blouse off in the next two minutes. He stopped here just to whistle at my lingerie. Cindy had helped me pick out some new items from a shop she knew in Greenwich Village. I had on a black lace bra with a front snap. I know I looked good in this, because I have nice breasts and this really showed them off. There was no top half to the bra so my nipples were openly visible. I had noticed different men staring at my blouse while we were out earlier. Cindy had also told me that men love stockings and hated pantyhose, so she got me some real nice black stockings that didn't need anything to hold them up. They were tight on my thighs but I had to admit I felt very sexy sitting in a short skirt with the tops of them showing when I moved. I also had black lace bikini panties. These did not last long.

Bill told me I looked great and pushed me back on the bed, for the first of many such falls I would take that year. I expected him to remove my bra and play with my breasts as he normally did, but he just unhooked it and reached for my panties. I told him to go slow because I was afraid. He told me to relax and slipped my panties down my legs. I was totally shocked at his next move. I expected him to get on top and enter me, but he knelt down and put my legs on his shoulders. I had no idea what was going on as he started to lick my pussy; I just knew it felt great. It had never occurred to me that men did this to women. I knew women sucked men's cocks and I was prepared to try this tonight, but I never realized that men also sucked women. I immediately wondered where he had learned to do this. That thought went out of my mind as soon as it entered because I was going out of my mind with pleasure. I think I would have had an orgasm if he had kept it up. (I didn't even know what an orgasm was then. I'm sure it would have scared me half to death.)

It wasn't too long when Bill stood up and unbuckled his pants. I wasn't scared anymore, because I was still trying to recover from my new feelings. Watching Bill undress was fascinating. I knew he was slim, with nice muscles, but I was surprised at how hard his body was. His stomach was flat and the little hair he had on his chest was fine like the rest of his hair, but it was browner than the hair on his head. I had heard the girls at school bragging about their boyfriends' cocks so I was curious about Bill's. It looked big to me but I had nothing for comparison. I knew it looked a lot bigger than the hole where it was going, so I was getting nervous again. Bill got between my legs and lifted them over his shoulders again. As he bent forward, my knees touched my shoulders. No one had mentioned anything like this at school. I was beginning to think that Bill was perverted.

I quit thinking about everything as his cock entered my pussy. It didn't hurt at all as it first went in, but then it stopped. I could feel him straining without gaining any more. I told him to back up a little and try again. He backed up almost out of me and then rammed me all at once. This hurt a lot. I

4

must have had a very pained look on my face as I lightly screamed, because he immediately pulled out and asked if I were all right. I recovered almost immediately and was determined to complete what we had started. I smiled and told him to try again. He entered slowly this time and slid completely into me. It smarted a little, but it was not a major pain like before. When he got all the way in, he stayed motionless for a minute and then began to pump me in slow strokes. I couldn't believe how good this felt. I immediately thought of some of the boys I had gone out with in high school and cursed myself for not giving in earlier. A few of them were real cute. While he continued to slowly fuck me, I began to notice all of the little things about him. I smelled his sweat mixed with the cologne. It seemed to intoxicate me. I still remember that smell to this day. I also noticed that I could feel his heartbeat under the fingers of my right hand. I had my hands on his back near his shoulders and I could clearly feel the blood pulsing through his veins. I never realized how alive a man could feel before this minute. All of a sudden I felt Bill stop moving and his body shuddered. I smiled as I realized that he was coming in my pussy. I could feel his cum splash against my walls.

After he came, Bill let my legs down and laid down next to me. The look in his face was wonderful. The look a man has on his face when he is totally sexually exhausted is one of the most satisfying looks a woman can ever see. I felt very female and very powerful.

I smiled back at him and told him "Thank you." He said he should be thanking me, but I told him that he made my first time wonderful, so it was only fair that I thank him. I didn't realize that I was fondling his cock as he was lying there until I felt it get hard again. Bill asked me if I was ready for another time and I nodded yes. This time was even better. He got on me and eased his cock into me. My pussy was still very sensitive. I had to stop him a couple of times before he got all the way in. This time he just lay still inside me for a longer period of time until I began to urge him to move. I noticed that he did not feel as big as when I had my legs over his shoulders, but I assumed that was because this was the second time in just a few minutes. Then he began to pump me with slow even strokes which slowly increased in speed until I was going out of my mind. When Bill came the second time, we were both too tired to immediately start up again.

I must have dozed off for awhile, because the next thing I remember is Bill licking my pussy again. I just lay there loving the feeling until I realized that he was eating his own cum out of me. I thought this was disgusting and told him to stop, but he told me to relax. He said any man that wouldn't eat a girl after he fucked her wasn't worth a damn. It was the first time I had thought about my being fucked. I had just thought of it as making love to Bill. I felt deliciously naughty about the idea of fucking instead of making love.

I decided to repay Bill for making me feel so great with his tongue. I slid down in the bed and grabbed his cock. I had never noticed before that it felt like velvet, but that was just how it felt as I felt along its length and down to his balls. I really loved playing with his balls as he lay next to me. It felt weird to feel them move between my fingers as I caressed

6

them. Finally, I got up the courage to put his cock in my mouth. It felt wonderful. I now know that part of what I tasted was my own cunt juices, but then I thought it was how all men smelled. He got hard as I took him in my mouth. My tongue seemed to automatically lick him as I took his cock deeper and deeper into my mouth. I had to stop because I felt like I was going to gag, but Bill put his hand on the back of my head and gently forced me to suck deeper and deeper. Soon I felt my nose touch his balls and I knew I had him all the way down my throat. He was getting very hard. I could feel his cock throbbing as my tongue licked it, and before I knew what was happening, he erupted a third time. I hadn't expected this and I gagged a little. I pulled away from him as he was still coming and ended up with his cum all over my face and hair.

Bill immediately apologized and kissed me. I didn't know what to say. I felt slightly used that he hadn't told me he was going to cum, but he said it came so quick that it surprised him. I wasn't too sure about this, but I didn't want to spoil the night, so I accepted what he said and again took him in my mouth. This time I could feel him get smaller and smaller. By the time he was completely soft, I decided that I really didn't mind very much, and made up my mind that I would swallow his cum the next time. I had heard some of the girls at school say they loved the taste of cum and some say they hated it. It tasted a little salty to me, but I didn't mind the taste very much. I just wasn't prepared for it. Next time I would be ready for him.

The next time didn't happen until morning. Bill said I had only slept for about fifteen minutes when I woke up and found him licking my pussy earlier. I slept almost eight hours before I woke up Saturday morning. Bill was upstairs in the shower. I was wishing he lived in a nicer place instead of this cheap boarding house because I wanted to get in the shower with him. I was embarrassed to even go up to the bathroom because I didn't know any of the other guys who lived in the apartment house. When Bill came back downstairs, he told me that no one was home yet or they were still asleep, so I went up to clean up. I hadn't brought a robe with me, so I wore Bill's. It was the first time I had ever worn a man's robe, and I felt very strange. I was just going back downstairs when some of the other boys came in. I felt like dying. They would know why I was there. I was sure that every man who ever looked at me again would know that I was not a virgin any longer. I must have been bright red as I went down the stairs, but the boys were real nice. They just said hello and continued on their way. I later found out that Bill fucked a lot of girls when I wasn't around so they didn't think anything about seeing someone new.

When I got back to the room, Bill was dressed and asked me if I wanted to go out for breakfast. I was starved. I hadn't noticed it before he mentioned it, and I was glad to have some place to go to get out of the building. We went over to the student union where the food was surprisingly good. By the time we were finished eating, I was feeling pretty good about myself. I thought about going back to the apartment again to use the bed, but then I thought about the other boys being there. Bill seemed to know what was on my mind, so he took me out for a drive. We went to a shopping plaza and he bought me a very sexy short nightgown. I think the saleslady thought we were newlyweds because she was real nice to us. By the time we got back to the car I was starting to feel sexy again, so Bill took me parking on a deserted road. I asked him why he bought the nightgown for if we were going parking, and he said that we had all night to enjoy the lingerie, but he wanted me right then.

This time I pulled his pants down first and then took off my panties. I kept my skirt on as I sat on top of him facing him, and eased his cock into me. Now there was no pain, only pleasure. I liked being on top like this. It gave me more control over my movements and I could concentrate on the feeling of him inside me as I fucked him. This was a novel thought. I never had thought of girls as fucking men, but that was exactly what I was doing. I loved the feelings, the feeling of his cock in my cunt, and the feeling that it was me fucking him instead of him fucking me. Even as I was fucking Bill, I knew that he wouldn't be the only man I fucked. I had already been out with a boy from Columbia in New York and I began to imagine it was his cock I was sitting on. I felt my body shudder a little as I was thinking this and Bill grabbed me and came as my cunt massaged his cock. He told me I was great. I couldn't help wondering what he would say if he knew I had been thinking of Steve when he was in me, but I just smiled and told him that he was great and I was lucky to have such a good teacher.

We went back to his apartment after this (Bill said everyone would be gone by now and I guess they were), and I put on my new nightie. I really liked it because it showed off everything that I wanted to show. My breasts were readily available and the hem barely came to the bottom of my bottom. Bill told me to forget wearing the bikini panties that came with it, so we just got into bed. I felt very grown up going to bed with a man in the middle of the afternoon like this. Bill again went down on me and worked me into a frenzy before putting his cock into me. This time he fucked me for well over half an hour. We were both totally exhausted when he finally came inside me. We fell asleep with our arms around each other.

About five o'clock I was having a great dream about making love to Steven (the boy from Columbia), when I woke up and realized that I actually was making love, but to Bill, not Steve. I must have had a very shocked look on my face because he stopped and asked me what was wrong. I said, "Nothing," and hoped that I hadn't talked in my sleep. Bill didn't mention anything I said, so I thought everything must be all right. Shortly after I woke up, Bill slammed into me real hard and came again.

Neither one of us was tired so we went out again to get something to eat. Bill took me to a nice little restaurant in town that had great chicken dinners. He told me to eat a lot because we were going out again and if I ate a lot, the alcohol wouldn't bother me as much. Cindy had told me the same thing at school, so I managed to have a really filling dinner. We then went back to Bill's apartment to change.

I put on the black bra that I had worn the night

before and the same stockings. I only had one pair of the sexy bikini panties, but then I remembered that I hadn't worn the panties that came with my new nightie. They were black just like my bra and stockings and they were certainly small enough to look like they belonged with the set. I picked out a blue blouse that showed off my tits and a very short gray miniskirt. The skirt easily covered my stocking tops when I was standing, but if I crossed my legs while sitting down, anyone could easily see the leg above the stocking. I felt very wicked. I knew that if I danced anything but slow dances, men could see the tops also, but Bill didn't like to dance so I wasn't worried about that.

We got to the bar where the band was at about nine-thirty. My nipples were easily visible through my blouse, and my cleavage was very visible. I'm sure half of the guys who saw me thought that I wasn't wearing any bra at all. I noticed that a lot of guys were stealing glances at me when their dates were not around. I felt great. I had never been this popular in high school. Bill and I found a table and ordered a couple of drinks. We hadn't been there very long before one of his friends came over and introduced himself to me. He said his name was Jack and he knew Bill wouldn't introduce anyone who looked like me to any male. I thanked him for the compliment and he sat down with us.

Bill didn't seem upset at all at Jack's inviting himself to sit with us. They were obviously very good friends. Bill encouraged me to dance when Jack asked me, but it was a fast dance and I knew my skirt was too short for that so I declined. We just sat around and talked for about a half hour. I couldn't help but notice how attractive Jack was, although he was totally unlike Bill. Jack was shorter, maybe five-eight, and had dark, almost black, hair. His face was rougher than Bill's. I don't mean scarred or anything like that, just much coarser than Bill's. In a strange sort of way, he was quite attractive. When a slow dance came along, Bill and I danced and then went back to find another round of drinks, our third, at the table with Jack. After a couple of more songs, the band played another slow dance and again Jack asked me to dance. I looked at Bill and he said, "Go ahead, Jack's a great dancer. You'll have a great time."

He was right. Jack was a great dancer, much better than Bill. He held me very close and moved with unbelievable grace. I got a little nervous when I realized that I could feel his cock getting hard as he held me closer, but then the music ended so we moved apart. As the next song started, Jack kept me on the floor to dance again. This was a fast song, but by now I had had three drinks and I wasn't so worried about my skirt flaring up. He was just as great a dancer on the fast songs as the slow ones. I glanced toward Bill and he smiled and waved at us. I stayed out for a third dance with Jack. This one changed pace so we ended up dancing slow again. This time I immediately felt his cock press against me. He maneuvered me so that I could feel it against my mound just above my pussy. I started to get seriously warm. When the song ended, we went back to the table and there was another round of drinks waiting for us. I was happy to see them because I was thirsty after dancing, and also because I was a little nervous.

Bill didn't seem to notice anything out of the ordinary, and all three of us sat and talked while the band took a break. We also ordered another drink. I normally do not drink much and this was the fifth within an hour. When the band came back Jack asked me to dance again, but I begged off because I had to go to the ladies' room. When I got back, Jack just stood up and guided me toward the floor. We danced two more fast dances. I realized that not only were the tops of my stockings showing, but anyone sitting near the dance floor was getting a good show of my tiny black panties. I didn't feel ashamed at all, but only began to get hotter and hotter. After the second dance Jack and I went back to the table with Bill. I was desperately thirsty and was glad to see that Bill had ordered just a glass of water for both him and me. I really didn't need anything else to drink right then.

We sat around and talked some more while the band played a few more songs. When they finally got around to a slow song, Bill and I went out to dance. He held me real close and I could feel his cock pushing against my mound. I felt like I was melting. I wanted to go back to his apartment and make love again. When we went back to the table, Jack suggested we go to his place and listen to his new records. I was surprised when Bill immediately agreed, because I knew he wanted to go to bed as bad as I did. I could plainly see the bulge in his pants when he was standing up. But he said he wasn't ready to go home yet and he was tired of everyone getting a free show when I danced. I was a little miffed at this because he was the one who told me to dance with Jack. No one would have ever seen up my skirt if I had only danced slow dances. I didn't say anything because he didn't really seem upset, and I wanted him to be as happy as I was. So we all got in Bill's car and went to Jack's apartment.

Jack's place was a lot nicer than Bill's, but then he didn't have a car so I guess they kind of balanced out that way. He immediately put on some slow music and went out to mix us some drinks. Bill and I danced real slow and tight until Jack came back with the drinks. We all talked some more as the music was playing. Then Jack stood up and grabbed my hand, obviously expecting me to dance with him. I looked at Bill and he smiled and said to go ahead. Jack again showed me what a great dancer he was. When the song ended, neither one of us started to sit down; we just stayed in each other's arms until the next song started. I could feel his right hand rubbing my ass as we stood there. (Bill had gotten up to flip over the record, and couldn't see my back.) When the music started again, we started to sway with it, but we never moved apart. His cock was as hard as a rock between us and my panties were soaked.

Bill said something about going to the bathroom, but I really wasn't listening. As soon as we heard the door close, Jack kissed me real hard, his tongue going in my mouth, and his hand cupping my breast. I returned his kiss and reached down and felt his cock through his pants. He whispered in my ear that he wanted to fuck me. I nodded agreement but said, "When? I have to leave early tomorrow." He told me that Bill was a poor drinker and would pass out within a half-hour. I couldn't believe this was happening to me.

When Bill came out of the bathroom, he came

14

over and put his arms around both of us. We were all swaying with the music. After a few minutes Bill said he was dead tired and was going to lie down in the bedroom for awhile. I thought he wanted me to go with him, but he told Jack to keep me entertained. I didn't know if I wanted him to go or not. I was super-attracted to Jack, but I really couldn't let him fuck me with Bill right here. I went in to see if Bill was all right and he said he was fine, just tired. Again he told me to have a good time with Jack. Then, as he was falling asleep, he said, "It's OK." I didn't know what he meant at the time, so I kissed him again and went out in the other room with Jack. We started to dance again, and this time Jack hardly had me in his arms before he started to kiss my neck and rub his hands on my ass and breasts. I started to respond immediately and grabbed his cock. I could feel it getting harder and harder as I rubbed it through his pants. I knew I was playing with fire as I unzipped his pants so I could feel it without his pants being between us. He wasn't wearing any underwear so his cock sprang out as soon as I freed it from its confinement. He was much longer than Bill. I told him to let me check on Bill again. I could hear him snoring when I got to the bedroom, so I went back to Jack.

Jack immediately took me in his arms and started unbuttoning my blouse. His cock was still out of his pants. I couldn't keep my eyes off it. Jack kissed me as he unhooked my bra and let it fall on the floor. I could feel my knees getting weak as he started to suck my tits. He kept sucking them as he was fumbling with the zipper to my skirt. Then he changed his mind and led me to the kitchen table. He bent me forward over the table and flipped my skirt up over my waist. I remember thinking how cold the table felt on my tits after his hot tongue had just been on them. I knew what was coming next, and I was not disappointed as he slid my panties down my legs. He didn't even lower his pants as he rushed to get his cock in me. I was a little nervous because I remembered it was so much longer than Bill's, but I had no trouble taking the entire length in one stroke. I just held on to the table and gritted my teeth so I wouldn't make any noise and wake Bill. I was becoming terrified that Bill would walk out and see us, but I couldn't have stopped this for the world. Jack didn't fuck me very long before I felt him slam as far into me as he could and flood me with his cum. I loved the feeling of his big balls slapping against my cunt as he fucked me this way and was sorry to have him quit.

After he rested a minute he pulled out and turned me around, rubbing my tits as he kissed me. I was still hot and greatly unfulfilled. I knelt down in front of him and started sucking his cock because I wanted him to get hard again fast. He did get hard again right away, but grabbed my hair, holding my head in place, and started racing in and out of my mouth. I knew he was going to cum in my mouth quickly, before he fucked me again, and he did. He came a lot considering he had just cum five minutes before in my cunt. I was proud that I swallowed every drop. I barely tasted him because he was so far in my throat when he came that it just went right down my throat without my having to taste it.

We went over to the couch to sit down for awhile. I continued to fondle his cock as we were talking. I

16

couldn't believe I had just done what I did, but I really didn't feel guilty. I must have known that Bill was screwing other girls. He was too good a lover to not be well experienced. He was definitely a much more considerate lover than Jack, who seemed mostly interested in himself. I noticed he made no effort to caress me for very long after he had cum the second time.

I decided I wanted him in my pussy once more before I went in to sleep with Bill, so I leaned over and started to suck his balls while playing with his cock. God, he had big balls, much bigger than Bill's. I had my left hand on his cock and my right was on his balls so I continued to suck them and lick his cock. I didn't even realize that my right hand was sliding down ever farther until I realized I could put my finger in his ass. I was rubbing nearer and nearer as I continued to suck his balls, when I finally put my finger in him. He got an immediate hard-on. This was what I wanted. As soon as it was totally hard I straddled him on the couch and lowered myself onto his cock. I was still wearing my skirt and stockings, but not my blouse, panties, or bra. I loved this position. It was a lot like screwing in Bill's car that afternoon. My tits were right at Jack's face so he was sucking them like crazy. He was squeezing my ass, causing me to move in a delicious motion on his cock. My mind seemed filled only with the feelings from my cunt. I couldn't think of anything at all.

I guess I couldn't hear very well either, because the next thing I knew Bill was standing beside me. I was terrified as I saw him there, but I couldn't stop moving. I must have closed my eyes for a minute because the next thing I remember seeing was Bill's cock right next to my face. I eagerly reached for it and put it in my mouth. I couldn't believe myself. Twenty-four hours ago I had been a virgin; now here I was sitting on my boyfriend's friend's cock with my boyfriend's cock in my mouth. Bill held my head with his hand as I was sucking him, but it wasn't necessary. I wouldn't have pulled my mouth from his cock if my mother had walked into the room. Now Jack had started to thrust upward with a lot of force and I knew he was going to cum again. He did just a few seconds later and I stopped moving as he shot up into me. Bill immediately thrust faster and soon he was coming down my throat just as Jack had done earlier.

As we all calmed down I started to get scared. I was still sitting on Jack's beautiful cock. I was afraid to get off, because then I would have to do something else, like talk to Bill and try to explain what had happened. Besides, Jack was still hard as a brick even though he had cum three times. I shouldn't have worried. As I was still sitting there leaned over on Jack, I felt Bill's hands start to massage my back. I realized he was doing this to relax me and I just let him continue. Soon Jack's cock began to shrink and finally it slid out of me. He kissed me hard, but I didn't kiss him back because Bill was right there. Bill leaned over and kissed my cheek and whispered that I should have kissed him back. I immediately did and Bill kept rubbing my back. Finally I stood up and turned around. Bill grabbed me and held me real tight as he kissed me over and over. I could feel Jack's hands lightly rubbing my ass as Bill and I continued to kiss.

Finally, Jack stood up and kind of guided us all to

the bedroom. He was tired from cuming three times in the last hour, but Bill was totally refreshed. I was placed in the middle and each of them sucked one of my tits and played with my pussy. I was becoming very aroused very quickly. Bill didn't wait very long before he moved down on the bed and removed my skirt and stockings. Then he put my legs on his shoulders like he did the first time and put his cock into me. Jack continued to suck on my tits and rub his left hand all over my upper body. He also french kissed me a lot. Pretty soon I heard Bill tel. him to stick his cock in my mouth, not his tongue. Jack complained that he wouldn't get hard again because I had already taken three loads, but he got on his knees next to me and guided his cock into my mouth. He was right. I couldn't get him hard again, but I enjoyed sucking him as Bill pounded into me faster and faster. Finally Bill came and collapsed on top of me. By now I had three loads of cum in my cunt and two down my throat, and I felt pretty wasted myself. We all slept until morning, with me between my two lovers.

When I woke up Sunday morning, it took me a minute to realize where I was. As soon as I remembered that, I remembered all that had happened the night before. I was afraid that I had lost Bill forever by behaving like I had, but before I could think very long I had to go to the bathroom. I didn't want to go back in the bedroom. I wanted to go sit and think for awhile, but my skirt and stockings were in the bedroom so I went back to get them. Bill was awake now and he reached up for me. I went over to him not knowing what to say or do. He pulled me down

19

on top of him and began kissing me. I wasn't really in the mood for more sex, but I did like the fact that he wasn't mad at me. Pretty soon I felt him get hard and start to push himself into me. I let him because I didn't really know how to say no after what had happened the night before. He rolled me over so I was right next to Jack and began to fuck me with long slow strokes. Despite my reluctance to start, I was beginning to like this and started to respond. There was no way Jack could stay asleep with the bed bouncing like it was. I was very embarrassed when he woke up and said, "Good morning." He leaned over, kissed my cheek, and got out of bed as Bill continued to fuck me. I heard the shower start as he went to the bathroom, and thought that he was not interested in sex in the morning. Bill continued fucking me all the time the shower was running and finally came shortly after the water shut off. We were both sweating heavily when Jack came back into the room. Bill got up and I started to follow him, but Jack said, "Not yet, Honey." He got on top of me in what I now know is the "69" position. At the time I didn't know what was going on, but when his cock was near my mouth, I started to suck it. He began to lick out my pussy like he was starving. Bill later told me that Jack loved to eat other men's cum out of girls. At the time I didn't think too much about it. After all, Bill had eaten me out after he fucked me so this didn't seem so much different. I just enjoyed it.

After we sucked each other for about fifteen minutes, Jack turned around and put my legs on his shoulders. In this position he went much farther into me than he had the night before. I now realized why

Bill favored this position. With his average-size cock, it enabled him to get in deeper than he would just lying on top of me. Jack went in so deep that I felt his cock hit bottom. Cindy later told me that he must have touched my cervix. He gave me a terrific fucking and we were both exhausted when he finally came. Bill had stayed and watched the whole thing, but I hadn't even been aware of his being in the room. After Jack and I finished, we all went and took a long shower together. Both of them got hard as I soaped their cocks, so I put a towel on the bottom of the shower, got down on my knees and sucked each of them till they both came in my mouth. I was very proud that I swallowed every drop. Bill later told me he was very impressed that I could not only swallow them, but actually get all of Jack's long cock into my mouth. I later found out that Jack was eight and a half inches long, which wasn't so terribly long, but I was the only girl they had had in Jack's apartment who was able to do it.

As Bill took me to the airport after breakfast, he told me he loved me. I asked him if he was sure after what I had done with Jack. He told me that was part of the reason he loved me so much. I didn't understand this at all. I had no desire to get into bed with another girl and share him at all. But he assured me he was telling the truth. He also told me he wanted me to be very sexually active in New York, and to learn all that I could. He said that if he had told me this after I had slept with only him, there would be indecision in my mind as to whether he were sincere, but the fact that he and Jack had shared me would convince me that he was telling me what he truly

21

believed. He said if we still loved each other after
having experiences with other partners, our love
could weather anything in the future, but if I did
nothing but stay home weekends and nights waiting
for mail from him, I would eventually resent his
power over me and we would drift apart. I wasn't too
sure about what he said, but as the plane took off I
couldn't help but smile while remembering my weekend. It was one heck of a weekend for a girl who had
been a virgin on Friday night.

CHAPTER 3
Back in New York

I landed at LaGuardia late Sunday afternoon, and
took a bus to the East Side Terminal and a taxi to
our dorm. (Our dorm was really an old hotel near
Herald Square.) All the girls were smiling at me as I
walked down the hall to my room. My friend Kathy
(still a virgin) couldn't wait to ask me what had happened. After I took a shower, I let her coax me into
telling her about Bill. I didn't have the courage to
mention what happened with Jack. She was shocked
enough that he had eaten me after fucking me. She
looked positively disgusted at that, but she wasn't
shocked by my sucking him at all. I showed her the
nightie that Bill had bought for me. She said it
looked "sluttish." I smiled and agreed with her. I was
wondering if Steve would like it.

Cindy got back late that night from a weekend in
Philadelphia. She also wanted a full report. She

asked me if Bill had liked the lingerie I had. When I told her he wasn't the only one, she was all ears. By the time I finished telling her about Saturday night, she was breathing heavily and fingering herself. I couldn't take my eyes off her hand at her pussy. When she told me to help her, I was glad to start rubbing her. When I sucked one of her breasts, she had an orgasm and had to put her arm to her mouth to avoid a lot of noise. We definitely didn't want any of the other girls to know what we were doing. After she came she hugged me and kissed me and asked me if I wanted her to return the favor. I wasn't prepared to do this, so I told her that I thought I had had enough sex for one weekend. She smiled and told me to wait for the next weekend. When I asked her what she meant, she said that she and I were going out to dinner with two of her friends. I told her that I would probably be going out with Steve on Friday night, but she said to make an excuse and postpone him until Saturday, or in her words, "Screw him before Friday, and he will gladly accept whatever you tell him about Friday."

I ended up doing exactly that. Steve called me Monday night and I told him I was going out with my girlfriends on Friday, but that I was free Tuesday night. He took me to a movie and then back to his room at Columbia. He shared a room with three other students in one of the buildings on Riverside Drive. We sat around for a while talking with the only one of them who was there, until he went to bed. Steve then started kissing me and fondling my breasts. That did it. I reached for his cock and started caressing it. He immediately got up and led me to the other bedroom. I hadn't worn my sexy lingerie this night, but he still stopped and admired me as we were undressing. I admired him just as much as he did me as he was undressing. Steve is even shorter than Jack, but he is very muscular. He also has a lot of hair on his body. I don't normally care much for hairy chests, but on him it looked fine. He is dark like Jack and has a devastating smile. The combination of his darkly tanned body, black curly hair, and brilliant white teeth is fatal to female virtue. I started to tell him how gorgeous he looked when he took off his briefs; then I just stopped talking and stared. He wasn't as long as Jack, but his cock was thick, real thick. I couldn't get my hand around it, not even close. I mentioned earlier how Bill's cock felt like velvet when I first sucked it. Well, Steve's didn't feel like velvet at all. It felt like an iron rod, a monstrous iron rod. I kept thinking that he was much too big to fit in me as he pushed me back on the bed.

Steve was much rougher than either Bill or Jack, but the head of his cock went into me without much trouble. We seemed stalled for a minute and he said he would take it easy because I was still a virgin. I blurted out that I was no longer a virgin. He had a shocked look on his face for just a minute and then pushed ahead. I felt my pussy expanding as he went deeper and deeper. God, he was big! I was thankful that he wasn't real long like Jack when I felt his balls hit my ass. After getting all the way in he stopped just a minute and then began to fuck me real hard. He came in just a couple of minutes, which surprised me, but he didn't get soft at all, which surprised me even more. The second time he pumped me for over

24

a half-hour before he came. One of his other room-mates came into the room for a minute while we were fucking and said to save some for him. Steve told him that I was only for him and to forget it. This made me feel super because I really liked Steve.

When he finished the second time, we lay on the bed talking. He wanted to know who had fucked me since he had last seen me. I told him about going home to see Bill, but I didn't tell him about Jack. I didn't want him to think I was a slut. He asked me if I enjoyed my weekend. I was honest and told him that I had a wonderful time, and Bill was a gentle lover who made my first time special. He looked a lit-tle hurt until I told him that although Bill was gentle he couldn't hold a candle to Steve's energy. Steve had fucked me hard, real hard, and I had loved it. "Besides," I told him, "you have a much bigger cock. A girl could get addicted to this." I grabbed his cock and slid my hand up and down it. He started to get hard again. I told him that I had to get back to the dorm. (We had hours at colleges in those days.) He said he would be quick, and he was. He put my legs on his shoulders just as Bill had done, and fucked me real hard again. I noticed that he got in me farther in this position just as Bill and Jack had. We actually moved across the bed because he fucked me so hard. True to his word, he came after about five minutes. Then he just lay on top of me for a few minutes and kissed me deeply. I was sorry I was going out with Cindy Friday night.

CHAPTER 4
Dinner with Cindy's Friends

When Friday night finally came around, Cindy had me dress in my sexy lingerie again. She told me the guys we were going out with were married and their stupid wives never dressed like this, so the guys would go nuts when we went to their hotel. I hadn't realized that the guys were married and I felt very uneasy about it. I told Cindy that maybe I should just stay home. After all, what did I have to gain by screwing married men. I remembered how hurt my mother had been when she found out my father had screwed her best friend. Cindy finally convinced me that we were not breaking up anybody's marriage, and the wives would never find out. We were just going to have a nice dinner and a terrific evening after dinner. She said she had already screwed both of the men and they were very good lovers. I was beginning to like good lovers and figured if she said they were good, I should believer her. So, I dressed as sexy as I could while still looking respectable enough for a nice restaurant. Respectable, I thought. Ha! Respectable girls don't go to dinner with married men, and they certainly don't go to bed with them. But I had to admit that I looked pretty good as I took one last look in the mirror as we were leaving. Cindy said Jim, my date, would be putty in my hands.

I felt strange walking into a bar in their hotel, the Hilton, but it didn't seem to faze Cindy at all. She just walked in and spotted them at a table right away. Both men stood up and introduced themselves to me before Cindy had a chance to begin introductions. Jim was a little like Bill in that he was kind of small of build and had fine features. Harry was handsome, but seemed rougher and much more authoritative. I don't know if that was just because he was taller or not. They both had on very expensive suits, so I felt somewhat out of place because I simply didn't have clothes that compared to theirs in quality. However, they didn't treat us like cheap girls at all. Like Cindy had said, they were perfect gentlemen, and after a short time I felt much more relaxed. We had one drink with them before they took us to the *Top of the Sixes*. I had never been to a restaurant in the top of a skyscraper before and I was duly impressed. I let Jim order for me, which seemed to impress him. Cindy had told them my background so he didn't order anything fancy, just a basic steak dinner, which was really great. What a difference from the normal food we had on Friday nights in the dorm. I thought right then that any girl who didn't accept a dinner invitation was crazy. I was more than willing to pay for it with a trip to the bedroom afterward. I did not have a lot of money, but I did know how to fuck, so it seemed like a fair exchange.

All during dinner, both Jim and Cindy's date, Harry, were perfect gentlemen. They asked me what I was studying, what I wanted to do and where I was from. Jim was a little shocked when we discovered he lived in a small city about twenty miles from my hometown. I must have had a worried look on my face, because he told me to relax, he had a lot more to lose than I did. This made sense to me. I really couldn't see him going home and telling everyone he had fucked Sharon Nelson in New York. His wife would find out and that would cause him a lot of trouble. I was beginning to think that Cindy was smart to go out with married men.

After dinner we strolled across 54th Street to Sixth Avenue, where the Hilton is. We were going to have another drink in the bar, but Harry suggested using room service. I thought this was great. I had never stayed in a hotel with room service before, so I felt very sophisticated when the waiter came up with two bottles of red wine.

We were still drinking our first glass when Harry and Cindy got up to go to the bedroom. (The men had a small suite.) I panicked a little at this, because now I was going to be alone with a man who fully expected to fuck me. Once again, Cindy must have told Jim how experienced I was, because he was very gentle as he slowly undressed me. He told me I looked great in my lingerie, and then started sucking my breasts. This is always my undoing. Once a man sucks my breasts, he's got me. I simply cannot refuse anyone who sucks my tits. Jim sensed this almost immediately and eased my panties down my legs. My legs parted to give him access to my pussy. Jim got down on the floor in front of me and started to tongue my cunt. This man was an expert. If they had contests for eating pussy, he would have had a gold medal. I started to breathe faster and faster as he continued to lick me and then my body simply shuddered in my first-ever orgasm. I must have screamed because Cindy and Harry came running out of the bedroom as I was catching my breath. Cindy asked me if I were all right, and I told her I was fine. She smiled when she saw me push Jim on his back on the floor and attack his belt. I had his pants down much faster than he had undressed me, and then I sat on his cock. I felt absolutely great. I leaned down to kiss Jim and could taste my juices on his lips. This seemed to inflame me even more and I started to move my ass so his cock was rubbing my insides in all directions. Jim now began to buck up into me with more and more force. I shortly came again and lay down on top of Jim. He was kissing me wildly and telling me how beautiful I was. I could feel his cock shrinking inside of me and almost cried when it finally slid out of me. I could also feel his cum slipping out of me and sliding down my cunt. Finally I lay down next to him on the floor and slowly regained my senses. He asked me if that was my first orgasm. I told him I had a very minor reaction before, but nothing like that. I really found it hard to believe that a man could do this to me. Actually, I found it a little scary. I liked the feeling of power I had had over Bill and Jack the previous weekend, but I knew I didn't have any power over this man at all. I would have done anything he asked right then. I still remember just gazing at him in total admiration.

I thought about Cindy's comment that Jim would be putty in my hands, so I thought I had better see what I could do for him. He seemed surprised when I moved down his body to take his cock in my mouth. He may have been surprised but he sure didn't complain. I must be a naturally good cocksucker because a lot of men complimented me on my technique long before I had enough experience to develop any technique. I eased Jim's cock into my mouth and heard him gasp when my tongue started licking as my mouth moved up and down. I noticed that his cock was about the same size as Bill's, so I knew that although I liked big cocks, I could have an orgasm with any man who treated me good enough. He was soon had as a brick again. This time he got on top and slid into me in one stroke. I wrapped my legs around his waist and moved with his rhythm. I didn't come again, but I had a wonderful time as he pumped me for over twenty minutes. I hadn't heard Cindy and Harry come out of the bedroom again, but after Jim came in me they both applauded. I had a silly thought and wondered if my mother had ever done anything like this, but immediately put it out of my head. I couldn't even imagine her being in bed with my father, let alone being with another couple.

After Jim and I caught our breath, we all had another glass of wine. I was surprised at myself for being able to sit with Cindy and these two married men wearing only my stockings. Everyone else was totally naked. I was a little self-conscious, but I thought I had a slightly better body than Cindy. Her breasts are smaller than mine, but her waist is too, so she is well proportioned. She's also about two inches taller than I am, so her legs are a little longer. I hadn't realized that her pubic hair was so much darker than the long blond hair on her head. My hair is the same shade of brown everywhere.

As we were finishing our drink, Jim was telling Harry how much he would enjoy me. Until that moment I had considered myself Jim's date for the evening and it hadn't occurred to me that I was expected to let Harry screw me. My face must have betrayed my shock because Cindy told me not to be so shocked. We were here to have fun with both Jim and Harry. Besides, she said, she was looking forward to Jim's famous tongue herself. I was more than a little apprehensive as Harry took my hand and led me to the bedroom. As I got to the door, I glanced at Cindy and Jim and saw her lean over to suck his cock. I envied her. I really liked Jim a lot, considering I had just met him, but I went into the bedroom with Harry.

Harry turned me around facing him and gave me a deep kiss and began to feel me up. As soon as he got my nipples hard with his hands, he bent over and began to suck them. This had the same result as it always has. He didn't have to push very hard for me to fall back on the bed. I was reaching for his cock as he continued to suck my tits as I lay on the bed. All too soon he got between my legs and started to ease his cock into me. He may not have spent much time warming up, but he had a bigger cock than Jim. As soon as he got the head in, he rammed the rest in in one stroke. I gasped with surprise as I felt his balls slap against my ass. My legs seemed to have a mind of their own as they wrapped themselves around his waist as he began to fuck me in earnest. I began to match him stroke for stroke as he continued to fuck me. My legs were tightening around his waist and I kept moaning, "Yes, oh yes. Fuck me. Fuck me." He did. I don't know how many times he had cum in Cindy, but he had great control. He just kept fucking and fucking. Finally, I heard Cindy shriek with pleasure in the other room and that seemed to send me over the top. My whole body tensed up and lifted right off the bed as Harry thrust deeply into me and held right there as he came. I could feel his cock throbbing as he pumped gobs of his white cum into me. His cock shrank fast and he rolled off of me and lay down beside me. We were both breathing hard and soaking wet from sweat.

When he leaned over and kissed me, he whispered in my ear that I was a great fuck. This was a new thought for me. I had never thought of myself as a fuck before, but I was pleased to hear that a man almost old enough to be my father considered me to be great. I kissed him back and thanked him, telling him that he wasn't so bad himself. Then I kissed him again to let him know that I really meant it, and told him that I was glad I got to fuck both him and Jim. He told me that he and Jim had been coming to New York for years and had screwed a lot of girls, but Cindy was the best they had ever had, and now she had introduced them to me, so she had some competition. I decided that I couldn't be that good because I hardly knew what I was doing.

Cindy had told me that she had been screwing on a regular basis for six years and had had well over three hundred men. I hadn't believed her when she told me this, but now I began to suspect she might be telling the truth. If a girl really liked to screw, as Cindy obviously did, and I was learning to, there was almost no limit to the number of men she could have if she was only looking for a good time. I thought of the strong feelings I had for Bill, but justified my present happiness by remembering that he had told me to get a lot of experience. Well, I had had three men since last weekend and it was only Friday night.

Cindy came in shortly after Harry and I finished and mentioned that we really should get going. The men had to catch an early flight and would need some sleep, "After all, a married man can't go home too tired to perform when he gets home, can he?" I hadn't even thought about leaving, but accepted what she said. I kissed Harry again and told him that I hoped I saw him again when he was in New York. On an impulse I bent down and gave his cock a lingering kiss. When I stood up I winked and told him that was just so he wouldn't forget me. He smiled and told me there was no danger of that, although he was having trouble remembering his own name right then. This made me giggle and I left with Cindy to find my clothes. After I dressed I went over to kiss Jim and told him to keep in touch. As I said this I reached down and squeezed his cock. He again told me that I was beautiful.

Cindy and I went downstairs and had the doorman hail us a cab. I felt very grown up and sophisticated. I wondered what my friends back home would say if they knew that shy Sharon had just had her brains screwed out by two married men in a major New York hotel. I was shortly to get the shock of my life. Cindy handed me a white envelope. I asked her what it was and she told me to open it and see. I opened it and found two twenties and a ten. I just looked at her in total confusion. She smiled at me and said it was a "present" from Jim and Bill. I was still shocked and said I couldn't take a "present" for what we did, but she insisted and told me they would be insulted if I didn't accept it. Then I thought I should split it with her, but she smiled and told me that she also had an envelope, and they had given her an extra "present" for introducing me to them. I was quiet the rest of the way home, but I put the envelope in my purse. I felt very strange.

CHAPTER 5
The Saturday After Payday

The next morning I again questioned Cindy about the "presents" we had received the night before. I told her it made me feel like a common prostitute. She said, "Honey, there is never going to be anything common about you. Your pussy is worth a million dollars if you use your head, so quit worrying about the $50. I know you can use it. Always, let me repeat that, always, accept a present from a man. If they are foolish enough to give us money and gifts for something that is readily available for free, we must be worth it. It was three years ago that a man first paid me and I thought that if someone was willing to pay me for something I loved doing, it was all right with me. Sharon, honey, you are good, you are real good. Be proud of yourself and keep the money. You didn't ask them for anything. They just gave it to you because they thought you deserved it. When a lawyer or an accountant performs a service for them, they wouldn't dream of not paying him. Well, take my word for it, the service you performed was appreciated a whole lot more than any briefcase full of legal papers or numbers. I heard Harry tell you that you were a great fuck. I've never heard him say that about anyone, not even me. I know I'm fairly easy to look at, but you were the one that Jim called beautiful. Those two guys are like money in the bank for you."

Now I was totally mixed up. I knew I shouldn't take money for sex, but as Cindy said, I hadn't asked for it. Like Cindy three years ago, I found it hard to believe that I could be paid for doing something that I so thoroughly enjoyed. I had a fleeting thought that I should be the one paying them. When I thought this, I didn't feel any different about them, so maybe they didn't feel any different about me now that I was just paid and not a special date. Then I blurted out, "They pay us because it takes away the guilt when they see their wives. This way we are never a threat to their family life." Cindy's right eyebrow shot upward when I said this and she said she had never thought of that before, but it probably had a lot of truth in it.

We went down to have breakfast with the other girls. Some of my friends were giving me a hard time about coming home so late last night, but I just smiled and told them that if they were having a good a time as I was, they wouldn't have come home early either. Of course they then wanted to know everything that happened. I told them about having dinner at the *Top of the Sixes*, which made them real envious, and the sex with Jim, but I didn't tell them about screwing Harry too. Besides, then they would have know that Cindy had also screwed both Harry and Jim, and that certainly wasn't any of their business. They were all a little in awe of Cindy because she seemed so much older than they did even though the difference was only three years. When we got back to our room, Cindy said she was pleased that I hadn't mentioned anything she had done. She really didn't seem to care if they knew, but she was pleased that I could keep things about other people to myself. She said this would help me a lot in the future if I continued to go with her on her "dates." Then she decided that we should go shopping.

She took me to a place on lower Madison Avenue that had really nice clothes. When I looked at the price tags, I must have turned white, because she asked me what was the matter. I told her that even with the $50 from the night before, I didn't have enough to buy any of these outfits. That's when she told me why she brought me here. First of all, she said never to spend more than fifty percent of what I made from sex, and to save all the rest. Then she said that the owner of this place was a really horny little old guy who would give us an outfit if he fucked us. This totally amazed me. "You mean we can have these clothes for sex?" I said. The price of the outfit I liked the most was over $200. Cindy said that we sure could, if we didn't abuse the privilege. We couldn't get over one a month, and we always had to come on Saturdays when the owner's wife was never here.

Just about then we were presented by whom I assumed was the owner. He was a "little old man" just as Cindy had described him. I was having trouble imagining having sex with him at all, when Cindy began to introduce us. I thus found out that his name was Saul. It had never entered my mind that I would ever have sex with a small unassuming man named Saul. She told him that I was following in her footsteps and was going to be a very wealthy young girl. I was getting nervous because he was staring at me as she kept talking about me. Finally she told him that there was one outfit that I really liked, and he asked her if I understood the terms of payment. Cindy told him that she had mentioned them to me, but hadn't given me the details. He told me to pick out the one I liked and try it on. I picked out a light blue suit that I really liked and went to try it on. I half expected him to follow me, but he didn't. He just remained talking to Cindy. When I came back out wearing the suit, they both smiled and said that I looked very attractive in it. Cindy said that I would be able to wear it anywhere and feel comfortable. She meant that it was expensive enough that I could wear it to dinner at the Plaza and not be embarrassed.

Saul now told Cindy to lock the door and put up the "Out to Lunch" sign. As she did this he steered me toward the back of the store to make adjustments. It was a little long for my taste. He agreed that it should be slightly above the knee and got his pins to mark the hem where I wanted it. He was all business as he pinned the hem and sleeves. Then he told me that was all and I could take it off. I looked at Cindy and she just nodded her head at me. I slowly removed the jacket and then unzipped the skirt. I wasn't wearing anything very sexy underneath because Cindy had only told me we were going shopping. I didn't know how I was expected to pay for the merchandise, but I guess I must have looked all right because Saul smiled as he reached behind me to unhook my bra.

After unhooking my bra he started to massage and suck my breasts. This had the desired effect and I began to get warm even though I was not attracted to him at all. I heard clothing rustle and saw that

Cindy was also getting undressed. She came over to us and told Saul to lie down on the floor because we were going to give him the treat of his life. She was unbuckling his pants as she was talking and started rubbing his cock through his underwear. By now he was pushing down my pantyhose while still sucking my tits. When he inserted a finger in my pussy, I was already soaking wet. He smiled at me when he discovered this, and sank to the floor as Cindy commanded.

Cindy had pulled his pants and underwear down to his ankles by now, so I got my first look at him without his clothes on. Unlike the rest of the men I had known the past week, he was older and not muscular. He wasn't real fat, but he didn't have that young healthy body I was used to. (Even Jim and Harry were in excellent shape although they were in their thirties.) His prick soon captured all of my attention. I gazed at it in surprise. He was almost as thick as Steve, but longer, like Harry and Jack. Cindy was sitting down with her pussy on his face and leaning forward to take his cock in her mouth. I wondered what I was supposed to do if she was sucking his cock and he was eating her pussy. Cindy soon motioned me to get down and start licking with her. I did and he was soon going out of his mind as both of our tongues were sliding up and down his cock. I liked it almost as much as he did because there was something about the smell of his cock and balls that seemed to get my chemistry into high gear. He had to tell us to stop because he was afraid he was going to cum too soon. Cindy sat up and began to really enjoy his tongue in her pussy. I straddled him and eased myself down on his big cock. I had had two as

38

long before and Steve was thicker, but I wasn't sure how easy it would go in. I shouldn't have worried. It went in to the balls with no trouble at all. I felt very filled as I began to ride his beautiful cock.

Cindy was facing me, still sitting on his face as I rode his cock. I felt her hands begin to softly rub my breasts. Pretty soon she leaned forward so that our breasts were pressed against each other and began to kiss me. I was unbelievably hot and I started pumping up and down on Saul faster and faster. He must have responded with his tongue to Cindy's pussy, because suddenly she grabbed me and screamed. With that Saul pumped up hard into me and I had an orgasm as I felt his cum splash against my pussy walls. My god, he came a lot for someone his age. I could immediately feel his cum easing out of my cunt, even though his cock was still hard and plugging my hole. He began to shrink shortly after this and I rolled off him and lay on the floor. Cindy lay down on top of him and licked his cock clean. After she was done she got up and started getting dressed. I immediately followed her and got dressed also. Saul had composed himself by now and told us we could have the suit by 4:30 that afternoon. (I was surprised at how fast it was done, but Cindy told me that he didn't want us picking it up when his wife was around. In fact, he didn't even want us in the store when his wife was around.)

Cindy now decided that we should have lunch. She said she would even let me buy her lunch, which seemed only fair to me. After all, she was responsible for my having both the new suit and the fifty dollars. She took me to a small restaurant on East 36th Street where the prices were quite decent for New York. As we were talking during lunch, I told her I thought it was strange that I had had orgasms with three men the past week, but they were all men who paid me in one way or another. I was somewhat worried about this. She told me to forget it because I didn't know the first two paid until after I had left them, and Saul always made her come too, even if she wasn't in a good mood. Besides, she was sure that I would come with Bill and Steve the next time I saw them. I decided to call Steve and see if we could get together that night.

When I told Cindy I was thinking of calling Steve that night, she asked me if I were still horny. I told her no, but I was interested to see if I would cum with him like she seemed to think that I would. Cindy was basically opposed to calling men to set up dates for sex (unless, of course, there was money involved), but she seemed interested to find out what I would do. So, after lunch we went back to our room and I called him. He wasn't home but one of his roommates said that he would be around tonight, and he would leave a message that I would be there. Instead of just saying goodbye, I told Andy to tell Steve that I would bring a friend.

CHAPTER 6
Saturday Night on Riverside Drive

Cindy looked at me in surprise when I told Steve's roommate to expect two of us. She asked me who I was taking with me. I told her I was hoping she would go. I knew she would love Steve's big cock and energetic fucking. If she couldn't go, I was going to ask Kathy. It was time she learned how wonderful it was to be fucked. Cindy didn't give poor Kathy a chance to find out. She said she would be glad to meet someone whom I liked so much, but she was a little surprised that I was willing to share him after he had refused to let his roommate fuck me. I told her I was looking forward to seeing if Steve could give her an orgasm. I was sure that he would give me one this time. After all, it seemed like almost anyone could who spent a little time getting me warmed up. Besides, I was proud of Steve. He was very handsome and I was eager to see his thick cock pounding in my friend. It seemed like I could start repaying her for all she had done for me this weekend.

The trip to the clothing store to pick up my new outfit was uneventful. Saul was busy with two customers and we had to wait for my suit. When he finally got to us, he was very nice and told me to stop in again anytime. I thought it was kind of cute when he patted my butt as we were leaving. After getting back from the clothing shop with my new outfit, we had a quick dinner at the school. I kept comparing it to the dinner that we had the night before. It didn't take long to decide that it was far better to let some handsome man buy me dinner than to eat what the school called food. My friend Kathy sat with us during dinner. I think she thought we were making up a story when we told her we were both going up to Steve's apartment for the night. She knew I really liked Steve and just couldn't see me sharing him with anyone, but I didn't feel any real competition with Cindy. I knew she wasn't interested in taking Steve away from me, she just wanted to have a good time.

This time I wore my sexy lingerie (not what Bill had bought me, but the half-bra and stockings). Even though I wasn't worried about Cindy being interested in Steve, I still wanted to be the center of his attention. I noticed that Cindy was also putting on some pretty fancy underwear. She had a bright red teddy and matching stockings that looked terrific on her. She also had some really sexy white garters to hold up her stockings. I thought these were really neat and made up my mind to spend some of my "earnings" from last night to get some. I asked her where she got them and she said the same shop in Greenwich Village where she had bought my bra and panties. Unfortunately it was not cheap, but if I were going to continue to fuck men for money, I would have to have a continual supply of attractive clothing, both lingerie and streetwear. This seemed to me like a reasonable cost of doing business. Besides, I assumed I wouldn't need too much new stuff because I would be working only very occasionally. I really couldn't see myself having more than one paying date a week.

But for how I didn't have to think about all of this. I was just thinking about Steve's big cock and hard pounding as I looked at how sexy Cindy looked in her teddy. I could feel my pussy getting wet just thinking about tonight. Cindy caught me staring at her and asked what was the matter. I told her nothing, I was only admiring how she looked and thinking about what was to come. She walked over to me and put her hand inside of my panties, feeling my wetness. She smiled and pushed me back on the bed and pulled my panties down. As she began to eat me I could feel myself getting real hot. I was super-disappointed when she quit after only five minutes of licking. I must have had the question all over my face because she said she only licked me to prime me for tonight. She had a feeling that it was going to be a night worth remembering. She pulled my panties back up and gave me a quick kiss. I could taste my pussy on her lips as I finished dressing. I wore a short green skirt and dark brown blouse. My mother would never have let me out of her house wearing a blouse without the top three buttons closed, but I wanted to feel sexy on my way up to Steve's.

On the way up to Riverside in the cab (Cindy wouldn't dream of taking a subway anywhere near Columbia University), Cindy asked me what I thought was going to happen tonight. I told her I didn't really know but I was sure she would have a great time. She said she was sure she would, but was curious to know why I had told his roommate that I was bringing a friend. After all, it was Steve she was interested in meeting, not his friends. I wasn't sure why I had told Andy I was bringing a friend. He was kind of cute and I guess I wanted Cindy to have something to do when Steve and I were alone together. I didn't really see Cindy and me in a three-some with Steve like we were with Saul. Oh well, I decided that whatever was going to happen would happen.

When we got to Steve's apartment, Andy opened the door. Andy's not really handsome, but he conducts himself with so much confidence that it is very easy to like him. He's a little taller than Steve, but not a lot; probably as tall as Bill. Unlike most of the boys in 1969, his hair wasn't real long. It wasn't cut real short, but it barely covered his ears. When he has his glasses on he looks really neat. Also he always smells great. He never has on too much cologne or too little. It's always the right amount. While I was introducing everyone, Cindy commented on the place being so nice. Steve said that with four people the rent was fairly reasonable for each one. All the time he was talking to Cindy, he had trouble taking his eyes off her. Even when he was talking to me, he had his eyes on her. As Andy was getting us some wine to drink, Cindy told Steve that she was interested in meeting him because I had told her great things about him. When he asked what kind of things, Cindy came right out and told him that I loved his big cock and the way it pounded into me. This brought conversation to a halt immediately. Andy stopped dead in his tracks as he carried the wine into the living room. Cindy looked shocked and said, "What's the matter? Don't you guys like sex?" They both immediately said that of course they did. Steve took her hand and pulled her to him. I watched as his hands ran all over her back as he kissed her. I started to get a little jealous when I saw Cindy's hand slide down off his chest toward his cock. Just as she began to massage it, Andy reached for me. I was still looking at Cindy and Steve as Andy began to kiss me. He must have noticed my open blouse, or maybe Steve had told him how my breasts responded to attention, because he soon had my blouse completely open and was unhooking my bra. Cindy and Steve were going into Steve's bedroom.

I was torn between following them and Andy's attention to my tits. When he began to suck my nipples my hesitation disappeared. I started returning his kisses with passion and reached for his belt. As I was unbuckling the belt and unzipping his pants he asked me if I wanted to use the other bedroom. I didn't say anything, but I got on my knees and pulled his cock free from his underwear. He had a nice cock. It wasn't as thick as Steve's, but it was a little longer and the head was much larger than the shaft. I swallowed the entire thing in one quick movement. I could feel it at the back of my throat as my tongue licked the shaft. I think he came in less than a minute as I grabbed his balls with one hand while using the other to pull him even deeper inside my mouth. He was so far in my throat that I hardly tasted his cum as it slid down my throat. I remember thinking that I wished I could get his balls in my mouth as well. I was licking them as he finished pumping his load in me. He was holding the back of my head so I could not get back from him as his cock very slowly softened. Finally, it slid out of my mouth and he joined me on his knees and started kissing me again.

I was starting to get seriously hot when we both stood up. He was again fondling my breasts, but this time he was also rubbing my ass. I knew he wanted to fuck me, but I was thinking about Steve and

Cindy again, so I suggested that we join them. Andy looked a little disappointed, but he didn't disagree with me. As we were walking toward the bedroom, he took my blouse and bra completely off so that when we got there I was half undressed. The first thing I saw as I looked inside was Cindy in her teddy and stockings in a 69 position on Steve. I was shocked when Andy immediately went over and stuck his cock in her cunt. This startled Cindy because she hadn't even seen us enter the room, but she just smiled at me as Steve continued to eat her while Andy fucked her. I went over and joined her on the bed. Steve's cock looked even bigger than I remember as I started to lick him. Cindy stopped her licking and began to kiss me as I engulfed Steve's cock down to his balls. I could feel her body rocking as Andy started to fuck her harder and harder. Suddenly she pushed me aside and sucked Steve again. I watched her body start to shudder and then stop. Steve must have cum right then, because Cindy began to gag a little and then recovered, taking all of his cum down her throat.

Steve was still hard when he finished coming, so Cindy said, "Be my guest," as she rolled off him and Andy slid out of her. I unzipped my skirt and threw it aside along with my panties, but I left my stockings on. I immediately started to sit on Steve's cock and take Andy in my mouth, but Andy said he had already had my mouth and he wanted to fuck me since the first time he saw me, so I turned around in the same 69 position that Cindy was in when we came into the room. I took Steve's hard cock into my mouth and put my pussy over his mouth. He just started to lick me as Andy rammed his cock into my cunt. I was having trouble concentrating on sucking Steve as Andy's thrusts became more and more forceful. Cindy noticed this as she recovered and began to lick his balls and cock like I had when she was on top. Finally she told me to move over because she wanted that big cock in her cunt. I rolled over on my back and Cindy lowered herself on Steve's cock. Meanwhile, Andy began to pump me harder and harder like he had Cindy. He was above me and slamming himself into me. The only part of our bodies that were touching were his cock and my cunt. I wrapped my legs around his waist as he kept fucking me. Part of the time my ass was completely off the bed as he pounded in and out of me. I could feel an orgasm building as he continued this for the next five minutes. Finally it came with blinding power. I must have screamed as his coming coincided with mine. My nerves in my cunt were so sensitive that I could easily feel every spurt from him hit my walls and the contracting of his cock as it continued to cum in me. It felt like he dumped a quart of cum in me. As soon as he stopped moving, I could feel it escaping from my pussy and running down my legs. Andy slowly grew smaller and smaller and slid out of me. He collapsed on top of me, totally exhausted. I turned to watch Steve and Cindy as Andy rolled over breathing hard.

They were just now turning over so that Steve could pound into her as Andy had just done to me. Steve was also supporting himself on just his arms as he started giving Cindy a terrific workout. His cock looked huge as it plunged into her over and over. I knew Steve wouldn't come quick because he had just come in her mouth a few minutes before. He didn't disappoint me. Andy and I were recovering and watching in fascination as Steve just kept pounding into her. I could feel myself getting warm again as I continued watching. Andy was behind me with an arm draped over me and fondling my breasts. I could feel his cock against my ass. It was slowly growing hard again. Every now and then he would kiss my neck, back, and the side of my face as I continued to watch Cindy and Steve. It seemed like we were watching for along time when Steve finally gave a tremendous lunge and froze. Cindy was actually whimpering by this point, but as soon as Steve started coming, she had another orgasm. It wasn't as strong as the one she had had with Andy in her cunt while she sucked Steve, but it seemed to leave her satisfied. Steve rolled off Cindy and lay down between her and me. I kissed him as he lay there, but he didn't have the energy to kiss back. He just smiled at me and continued breathing hard.

Andy got up and said he was going to get the wine we had hardly tasted. While he was gone Cindy recovered and told me that I hadn't exaggerated at all when I bragged Steve up, but I hadn't mentioned anything about Andy. I told her that until a few moments ago I hadn't known anything about Andy. I was looking at Steve when I was saying this because I still remembered that he had told one of his roommates last Tuesday that he wanted me just for himself. Even though he had just fucked Cindy, I still didn't know if he would like me after he saw Andy fuck me. He was breathing more normally now and asked me why I had brought Cindy up to meet him. I told him I was very proud of him and Cindy had wanted to meet someone I had talked about so much. I said I hadn't known Andy was going to fuck me until he and Cindy had gone to the bedroom together, and even then I wasn't sure until we joined them. "Besides," I told him, "when I started to get on your cock you didn't say anything when Andy told me to get in a 69 position over you so he could fuck me. So, I assumed you didn't care if he fucked me." And, I said, "When we came in the bedroom, Andy just went over and started fucking Cindy as you were eating her, so I think you two have done this type of thing before."

Steve was a little taken aback by my quick response, but he admitted I was right. They had done this before. I suddenly thought of Bill and Jack sharing me and realized they must have done it a lot before too. Andy had come back with the wine by now, so we all sat up to have some. After we had all had a glass, Cindy asked us if we wanted something to smoke. Steve and Andy immediately said yes, but I said I didn't smoke. They all seemed to have a good laugh at my expense here and then I realized that they were talking about a marijuana cigarette. I had never had any drugs at all and I really didn't want to start now, but I let myself be persuaded. I think Cindy did it when she told me that the sex would be even better. I couldn't believe sex could be better but I was interested in finding out. I watched the three of them smoke before I tried it. Even then I coughed the first couple of times I tried inhaling the smoke, but I did begin to feel lightheaded. I also began to get warmer. Taking another glass of cold wine didn't seem to decrease my temperament at all. Pretty soon I was totally engrossed in watching

Steve's cock grow. It looked huge as it kept growing. Cindy had also noticed and reached over to rub it with her hand. Andy was getting interested by this time and was sliding her teddy down from her tits. As he began to suck them, Cindy quit playing with Steve and reached for Andy's cock. Steve now rolled over on me and rammed me with his cock. I actually screamed because he hurt me with his force, but he didn't slow down at all. He just began to fuck me like a wild man. I hadn't realized how strong he was until he picked me up from the bed and kept fucking me standing up against the wall. My legs were wrapped tightly around his waist and I was holding on for dear life as he continued to pound into me. It wasn't long before I could feel an orgasm building. Every nerve ending in my cunt was on fire from his furious fucking and I screamed out again, but not in pain, just the pleasure of high-powered fucking.

He carried me back to the bed and almost threw me onto it as I was still coming. I almost cried when his big cock left me. I wanted him to just stay inside and rest with me for awhile. This was not to be. He roughly pushed my legs apart and started fucking me again. This time he began taunting me, whispering to me that I was a little slut, because I fucked Andy so quick and came so easily. Cindy and Andy were too interested in each other to pay any attention to us, and he kept calling me names. He said he bet I'd like even more men that night, and I liked being a slut. More men hadn't even entered my mind. My cunt was getting sore from his fucking and he was still fucking me. I was literally bouncing off the bed as he pumped me without mercy. I started to kiss him real hard just to shut him up. Finally he gave a huge lunge like he had with Cindy and froze. I felt the hot cum spurting into me. My back was arched as he held my ass off the bed while he continued coming. Between the two of us, only his knees and my shoulders were on the bed. As he held me in this position, he began to move in a circular motion that made his cock seem even bigger. My cunt felt like it was getting totally stretched out. He eventually began to get soft, thus bringing me some respite. Finally he let me lie back on the bed and he lay down beside me.

I had a lot of thoughts running through my mind about what he had just said as I lay there. Where did he get off calling me names? He had admitted that he and Andy had shared girls before. Why was it any different for me to enjoy both of them? He obviously enjoyed fucking Cindy. Why shouldn't I enjoy fucking Andy? Thinking of Andy I looked over at him and Cindy. The bed was still moving from their fucking. Andy was on top of her and she kept telling him to come in her, and that she wanted his cum in her. I gave Steve a dirty look and told him that if he thought I was a slut, I may as well act like one. I went over and knelt behind Andy. I saw Andy glance at me, wondering what I was going to do. I just watched Andy's cock going in and out of Cindy for a couple of minutes. Cindy was still talking to him, saying, "Come, damn you, come." I leaned forward and licked his balls. He quit pumping so hard, and changed to a shorter stroke so I could keep licking. I suddenly remembered how quick Jack had got hard when I put my finger in his ass. I slid my finger up Andy's ass. It had the desired effect. He rammed into Cindy just once more and froze. I saw his balls

51

tighten up just before they came. I kept licking them until they started to loosen up again. Finally, Andy pulled out of Cindy and backed up. As his cock came free I had a sudden desire to lick Cindy's juices off it. I promptly fulfilled this desire. Andy laid back on the bed as I licked him until he was totally soft.

Steve had naturally watched the entire time I licked Andy. I don't think he knew what to think. I'm sure he still didn't think I was a virgin until just a week ago. He was sure looking at me in a strange way. He didn't seem to despise me, but I was sure he would never consider me the type of girl he wanted all to himself again. I felt both a little sad and a little freer. I liked having him like me so much that he wanted me all to himself, but I knew it was silly to have two serious boyfriends. I knew my relationship with Bill was pretty solid. I believed him when he told me that he expected me to get a lot of experience while I was in New York. Why else would he have let his friend fuck me? Actually, he almost pushed us together. I couldn't believe he would do that if he hadn't wanted me to have other men.

While I was trying to figure out my feelings toward Steve, we all heard other people come into the apartment. Steve and Andy immediately recognized the voices as Les and Bob, their other two roommates. I had never met either of them before so I was a little concerned when they asked if everyone was decent. Andy said, "Decent? These two girls are fucking fantastic." As soon as he said that, Les and Bob both came into the bedroom. I hadn't heard any female voices but there were two girls with them as they came in. I was embarrassed to be seen by four total strangers in a bedroom with two men and another girl while I was only wearing my stockings. Strangely enough, I was more embarrassed by being seen by the two girls than the two boys. Cindy's teddy covered her up pretty well when she crossed her legs (it had obviously been unsnapped early in the evening), but my breasts were totally bare. One of the girls had a totally shocked look on her face but the other one didn't seem surprised at all. She (Lorraine) turned to her friend and said, "See, Lisa, I told you these guys really know how to have a good time." Lisa just looked scared. I couldn't believe how much older I felt than she looked, but we must have been the same age.

Les and Bob were both staring at Cindy and especially at me. When they came in the room I was sitting on the floor between Andy's legs with my hand on his cock. It was very obvious what I had been doing, but Cindy was just lying on the bed. Finally, Andy stood up and said hello to Lorraine, pointing out that he didn't know Lisa at all. When he stood up, his cock was just above my nose. The very smell of all the sex seemed to intoxicate me. I reached up and started sucking his cock again. He said, "See, I told you these girls were fantastic. Sharon here is a changed woman. She just can't stop." Les said that he thought I was Steve's girl. Andy told him that "was" was the operative word there. I was now a full-fledged party girl for all of them to enjoy. Steve had now gotten up and was telling Lorraine it was good to see her again. Cindy had decided to join the conversation and started unbuckling Les's belt. Lorraine reached down to take Steve's cock in her hand, and told him that it was good to see him again too. Andy pulled out of my mouth and said he was going to get some more wine and ice. Bob came over and told me not to look so disappointed. There were plenty of cocks, so I didn't have to worry about losing Andy's.

I was watching Lisa as Bob lowered his pants and pulled out his cock. She was evidently with Les because she was watching Cindy's progress with his pants very closely. I could see her breasts start to heave and her breath coming faster. I thought she had never done anything like this before, but she was certainly becoming aroused. She saw me watching her and realized she was the only inactive person in the room. Just then Andy came back with the wine. I told her to have a couple of glasses and join us. Bob's cock was getting hard right in front of my face so I took him in my mouth. She turned to Lorraine as her only friend in the room just as Lorraine's blouse came off. Her bra immediately followed and Lisa stared at her tits as Steve took one in his mouth. Her eyes then went to Steve's cock. It was getting hard again, and she was obviously fascinated by its size. I took Bob's cock out of my mouth and asked her what was the matter. I was beginning to think she was a virgin. She said, "I've never seen anything that big before." I told her he wasn't really big, only thick, but he was a great fuck and I was sure she would enjoy him.

By now Lisa had drunk a glass of wine and seemed a little more relaxed. Andy took her glass from her and began to kiss her. She looked for Les, but he was busy crawling on top of Cindy in the 69 position. As soon as he started to lick Cindy he said, "My God, this girl's full of cum!" Then Cindy wrapped her legs around his head so he couldn't have escaped even if he wanted to. Lisa turned back to Andy and started to return his kisses. Her hand slowly found its way to his cock. As soon as she touched his cock, Andy was hard again and started removing her clothes. Within three minutes she was completely nude and falling on her back. Andy stayed with her and entered her as soon as she hit the bed. Bob was tired of just standing there in front of me so he grabbed my head and put his cock in my mouth again. I swallowed him to the hilt with no problem. He came as I started to use my tongue to lick the shaft, but he never got soft. I got off the floor and on the bed. My head was next to Lisa's, but my pussy was right at the edge of the bed. Bob put his hands under my ass to raise me a little bit, but his cock kept missing my cunt. I couldn't believe it was possible to miss it after all the fucking it had had tonight. I thought it must have been a huge target. Finally, I got tired of Bob's attempts to enter me and guided him into my cunt. I was surprised when I could feel his shaft inside of me. I thought I would be so loose that I wouldn't be able to feel anything, but I felt just like I had earlier in the evening when Andy first fucked me. However, Bob's cock was just average. It didn't have the huge head that Andy's did. But it still felt good as he continued fucking me. He used a circular motion like Steve had done, which made him feel bigger than he was, and made me feel great.

Andy was still fucking Lisa with a slow steady pace. I leaned over and kissed her cheek as I watched them. She was startled by this and looked at me very strangely again. I smiled at her and whispered, "He's good, isn't he?" I hadn't wanted Bob to hear me when I said this and I don't think he did, but shortly afterward he pulled out of me and went over to Cindy, who was still sucking Les. Bob pulled her down so that her cunt was at the edge of the bed and entered her in one stroke. I noticed that he didn't need any guidance to get into her. As soon as Les opened his eyes and realized that Cindy was being fucked, he noticed that no one was with me, so he came over and started fucking me. Lisa seemed relieved that Les was fucking someone else. I wasn't sure what their relationship was, but I thought that she probably came here tonight expecting to spend the night with Les. I knew she hadn't expected to watch as a total stranger started sucking his cock, and to fuck a total stranger herself. She asked me how he was, and I told her that he was doing a fine job. Just then Andy started slamming into Lisa real hard and came again. Les was obviously very interested in watching Lisa. He was hardly paying any attention to me. I told him to go get her. She obviously wanted him. He left me and walked around the bed so he could get between her legs. I heard him saying something to her but I couldn't hear what it was. I did hear him say slut just as Andy put his cock in my face. I decided I didn't like Les very well. I again sucked Andy as he went soft. Lisa's juices tasted different than Cindy's, but I liked the taste of both. Finally, Andy lay down next to me and we just watched the action.

Steve was fucking Lorraine by now like he had me earlier. He was standing up as he held her against the wall. She was practically begging him, "Come on Steve, fuck me harder! Harder! You can do better than this. Watch Bob, he's fucking your friend Cindy

56

real well. Watch her move. Come on, fuck me!" It occurred to me that she thought that Cindy was Steve's date for the night because I had been with Andy when she first walked in the room. I had to admit that Bob was doing a fine job on Cindy, far better than he had done on me. Les was now leaning over Lisa and I heard him whisper to her that he couldn't believe that his roommate fucked her before he had. She told him that he was somewhat busy at the time that Andy took her, and she was hot from watching everyone else in the room. Les fucked her hard for a few more minutes and then came in her. Lisa was breathing hard, but I noticed she hadn't had an orgasm with either Andy or Les.

After Les pulled out of her, Lisa got up to go to the bathroom. I got up with her and asked her to show me where it was. I liked her and wanted to talk to her for a minute. She was shy again as we left the bedroom, but began to talk when we were alone. I told her I thought she hadn't done anything like this before. She told me she had only been to bed with two boys before, and that was over the course of her senior year in high school. She was totally shocked when I told her that until a week ago Friday, I had been a virgin. She said I seemed so at ease with more than one man, that she thought I had had a lot of men.

Then she said, "Didn't Les say you were Steve's girlfriend?"

I told her I wasn't sure anymore, but I thought I was when I came up here tonight. She asked me what I meant, and I told her that Steve had been really nasty to me earlier.

"You mean like Les was to me a few minutes ago?"

"Worse, he kept calling me names and had a real nasty tone in his voice. I don't really need anybody giving me any crap all the time. So, I guess I probably won't be seeing much more of Steve. Besides, I kind of like Andy now. I didn't know him before tonight, but he seems nicer than Steve."

Lisa agreed that Andy seemed nice. She giggled when she also mentioned that he was a better lover than Les. I agreed with her that Andy was a good lover, but I told her that before the night was over, she should let Steve screw her because he was a great fuck. And I reminded her I had seen her staring at his cock when she came into the room. She blushed when I said this and told me that she had never imagined that men were that thick, and she couldn't see how it would go in her. I reminded her that she had seen Steve and Lorraine fucking in the bedroom a few minutes ago, and Lorraine certainly didn't act like she was in pain. I could almost see her thinking of that as she asked me for my address and phone number. I was glad to see she wanted to be friends and quickly exchanged information with her. We then went back to the party. I hoped Steve had enough energy left to fuck Lisa like he had Cindy and me.

I shouldn't have worried. Steve and Les were both hard again from watching Andy screw Lorraine and Bob screw Cindy. When Bob pulled out of Cindy, Les immediately climbed on her and rammed his cock home. Cindy just smiled and kept moving. Now Steve and Bob both started kissing Lisa while I just sat on the bed and watched. Lisa was a little uptight at first, but she relaxed more as they pushed her back on the bed. Bob knelt in front of her pussy and began to lick it as Steve brought his prick to her mouth. She slowly began to lick and kiss it. I think the smell of Lorraine's sex on it must have inflamed her, because all of a sudden she began to swallow it. She seemed like a woman possessed. Bob stood up and began to fuck her as she sucked Steve faster and faster. After about ten minutes, Bob said, "Let's switch," and they did just that. Bob came over to her mouth. Lisa looked a little disappointed because he was so much smaller than Steve, but she took him in her mouth to the balls with no problem. Steve lifted her legs onto his shoulders and eased his cock into her in one stroke. Lisa pulled away from Bob for a minute and said, "Oh, my God. He's huge!" Steve now began to fuck her in earnest. He was picking up the tempo as she went back to Bob's cock in her mouth. By now Lorraine had finished with Andy and took Bob's hand and led him to the floor where she proceeded to ease his cock into her cunt. Andy's cock was soaked from its turn in Lorraine and was rapidly shrinking. He came over to me, but we both were too tired to do much except watch the action.

Even though I was still angry at Steve for what he had said earlier, I was impressed by the way he was fucking Lisa. After all, she was the fourth girl he had fucked that night and he was pounding into her almost as hard as he had in Cindy and me. Lisa was literally bouncing off the bed as she screwed her. Andy and I continued to watch and we slowly started to become aroused again. He began to fondle my breasts and I was rubbing my hands over his chest and stomach. I finally worked my way down to his cock and balls, but he simply was not going to get hard again. As I was fondling his cock, I heard Lisa tell Steve to come because she was getting sore. I whispered to Andy that I was going to help Steve come and got on my knees behind him as I had with Andy earlier. As I licked his balls, I couldn't help but be overwhelmed by the smell of sex from Lisa's cunt. I watched in fascination as Steve's big cock stretched her. Remembering what I was here for, I again licked his balls. I could feel them tightening as he started to move even faster, so I worked my finger in his ass just as I had with Andy. It had the desired effect. Steve gave one more powerful lunge and started pumping his cum into her. It was leaking out of her almost immediately and running down her ass onto the bed. When his cock finally slid out of her, I took it in my mouth as I had Andy's earlier. I loved the taste of Lisa's juices mixed with Steve's cum as I licked him clean. While I was taking care of Steve, Andy had begun to caress Lisa. He slowly brought her breathing down to a more normal state. I felt a pang of jealousy as Lisa leaned over to kiss him. I think she enjoyed Andy's attention as much if not more than Steve's fucking.

That was the end of the sex for the night. Andy went and got us some more wine. Even Cindy seemed totally wiped out from all the activity of the evening. After we got dressed (boy, did I have a hard time finding all my clothes), we had another glass of wine before leaving. I went back into the bedroom to say good night to Steve and Andy and was surprised that Lisa was still nude and on the bed. She smiled a weak smile at me and said it was a little late for her to be getting back to her dorm. Then she sat up, kissed me on the cheek and told me to call her. I kissed her back and told her that I would. Cindy and I left then to get a cab back downtown.

CHAPTER 7
Two Quiet Days

Cindy and I did next to nothing on Sunday except study. It probably seems hard to believe from what I've written, but I was going to college and I did have a lot to do. Cindy did mention that I seemed to have made a new friend. I said that I did like Lisa a lot and hoped to get to know her better. Monday was a full day for both of us at school and I had a lot of work to do that night. Cindy had to go to the library that night, so she wasn't home when Rachael called. Rachael sounded disappointed that Cindy was not around and asked me to have Cindy call her back.

When Cindy got home, she returned Rachael's call. I heard her mention my name, but didn't think anything about it. After she got off the phone, she told me that Rachael wanted to meet me. I asked her who Rachael was and was surprised when she told me Rachael was the madam who set up the dates for us last Friday. I guess I had just assumed that Cindy had done all of this herself, but she told me that Rachael ran one of the most exclusive escort services in the city. I didn't even know what an escort service was until Cindy explained everything to me. She said that some men only wanted companionship when they were in the city and the services provided that. Rachael's was more exclusive in that it provided sex as well as companionship. Rachael also ran a classy "house" on the Upper East Side.

I was extremely interested in what Cindy had to say. I had never even thought of things like this before. Oh, I had heard the term "call girl," but I never really thought about it. I saw hookers on the streets every day and definitely didn't want to end up like them. But Cindy was different. It occurred to me that she was a call girl, at least part-time, and by accepting money and presents Friday and Saturday, I was on my way to becoming one. I didn't know about this at all. Being a call girl was not what I was going to college for, but I certainly liked the extra money. I asked Cindy why she was going to college if she could make so much money working for Rachael. She said that she couldn't work for Rachael all her life, and besides, the men she wanted to "date" appreciated a woman who had gone to college. "Smart men do not like stupid women, Sharon." I have thought about those words many times over the last few years and I have to agree that she was definitely right. There are a few intelligent men who like dummies for sex, but they are all too insecure to interest me anyway. I like secure and intelligent men. Of course it doesn't hurt anything if they have money. I decided to go meet Rachael with Cindy on Tuesday afternoon.

CHAPTER 8
A Meeting with Rachael

We both were done with classes by three o'clock on Tuesday afternoon so we changed into nicer clothes (and good lingerie) and took a cab to a brownstone in the east seventies. This was certainly a beautiful area of the city. Everything was well kept and clean, and all the people looked at least well-to-do if not rich. I later found this was only the way they looked. A lot of these people were working very hard and spending everything they made to keep up appearances.

When Cindy rang the bell on the brownstone, the door was opened by a maid. I don't know why this shocked me so much. I guess I just never thought of people in this "profession" having servants. I kept thinking of the girls on the streets when I thought of receiving money for sex, but those girls were never going to live like Rachael did. The maid smiled at Cindy and called her by name. Cindy introduced me to Maria (who was from Puerto Rico, but I couldn't hear any trace of an accent), and then Maria took us in to see Rachael.

Rachael was a truly lovely woman. She was in her early forties (Cindy had told me this), but she was outstanding. It wasn't so much that she was beautiful as the class she had. She acted like she had been born rich and charming. I had kind of thought that I would be having an interview, like a job interview. I suppose it was, but I didn't feel uncomfortable at all. Rachael got up and came to meet us when we entered the room. I have never been on a legitimate job interview where this happened, and it put me at ease right away. She led us to a very comfortable L-shaped sofa where there was no desk in the way.

Rachael was aware that Cindy had taken me along on her date with Jim and Harry Friday night, so she asked me how I felt about receiving money for sex that night. I told her that I was glad that Cindy hadn't told me about being paid before we went out, because I know I wouldn't have gone if she had. Rachael asked why not, and I told her that I had been brought up in a small town where sex for money was virtually unknown and highly disapproved of. (I purposely avoided the use of the word prostitution.) Even pre-marital sex was thought to be terrible. She then asked me if I was sorry that I went. I had to truthfully tell her that I wasn't sorry at all. I even told her that I had my first orgasm that night, and that I had enjoyed myself immensely. When she asked me if I thought I could do it again knowing beforehand that I would be paid, I answered yes. She said that she wanted me to understand that everyone was not as nice as Jim and Harry, but she didn't have any clients that hurt girls or mistreated them. All of her business was from referrals, so the men were screened before she ever met them. No man who wanted to continue using her service would recommend another man who mistreated the girls. I told her she probably had a lot nicer class of men for clients than most girls would be going out with, if we just were on dates.

She smiled broadly when I said this. Then she suddenly asked what I did with the money Cindy gave me. I truthfully told her that I had saved all but ten dollars. I had put forty dollars in the bank on

Monday. I definitely did not mention going "shopping" with Cindy on Saturday. (Cindy had told me that Rachael didn't know about Saul, so I had to keep my payment for the suit a secret from her.) Rachael was very impressed that I had not spent all of the money. She said she always tried to impress young girls that they could not do this forever, so they should save half of what they make, but so few did. She suddenly got more businesslike.

"Well, from what I understand, you would be willing to work for us on at least a part-time basis, is that correct?"

"Yes." I heard myself saying this before I even thought about it, but I knew I could fuck any man this woman wanted me to, and I would probably be glad to do it.

"Good. If you work here in the house, you get half of whatever the customer pays, plus any tip he may want to give you. The more you do the more you'll make. If you go on dates, I normally take a flat fee of $100 and let you keep whatever else we charge him. By the way, did you suck the men last Friday?"

"Yes. I've sucked every man I've gone to bed with."

"That's good. You really can't work in this business unless you are willing to suck cocks. Tell me, Sharon, how many men have you slept with?"

I had to stop and count before I answered. I started naming them out loud. "Let's see. There was Bill, Jack, Steve, Jim and Harry, Andy, Bob, and Les. Eight." I knew I had left Saul out, and noticed that Cindy was relieved that I hadn't slipped up and mentioned him.

"Well, you've been a busy little girl, haven't you?

Cindy told me you were a virgin less than two weeks ago."

"I guess I just like sex. I like it a lot. All day Monday in class, I kept looking at men's crotches and wondering what they had inside their pants. I'm real lucky that there's the pill now. I'd have probably gotten pregnant if we didn't have it."

"Are the payment terms all right? Do you think you are being treated fairly?"

"Half seems fair to me, but what did you mean when you said the more I did the more I would make. I realize that if I have a lot of men I would make a lot of money, but that's obvious."

"That's right, that is obvious. What I meant was the more things you do sexually, the more money you will make. You do like to suck cock so you will have no trouble there, but if you want to make the really big money it helps to be a little kinky. I have one girl who specializes in handcuffing and whipping men. She is a very busy girl, and she makes well over a thousand dollars a week and never works more than three days. But this is not something that someone your age normally will even consider."

I had to agree with that last statement, but I didn't know what to say about her next sentence.

"However, most girls eventually do give in and have anal sex."

My eyes must have gave away my feelings totally because she immediately started to reassure me. "Honey, you don't have to have anal sex. There are plenty of men who will be very happy to fuck only your mouth and cunt. However, men will pay at least twice as much for the privilege of fucking your ass. But don't worry. You can do whatever you want."

66

"Well, I think we can forget the anal sex, but I would love working for you. How do I get started?"

"If you want, you can have someone this afternoon."

I hadn't expected to be told this. I really liked the dates like Cindy and I had Friday night, but Cindy jumped in and said we had come "dressed" for work. Then she told me to show Rachael how I looked. I was surprised at this, but Rachael seemed to expect me to show her. I had worn my most expensive black bra and panties and a new pair of black stockings. When I removed my jacket, blouse and skirt, I could see that Rachael was pleased. She told me that I would be very popular with any man who still had life in him. As she finished talking she came over to me and unhooked the front hook on my bra, feeling my breasts. She was murmuring how nice they were when she began to suck them. I think she was very pleased that I did not withdraw, but started to respond. She kept sucking me as her hands travelled down to my pussy and removed my panties. Cindy had come up behind her and started removing Rachael's clothing. Rachael gently pushed me to the floor and got on top of me in the 69 position. As soon as she started to lick me I returned the favor. Her cunt smelled delicious as I put my mouth to her and began to eat her. She was of course the more experienced and soon had me coming on her tongue. While I was coming I stopped eating her and Cindy knelt behind Rachael and took my place. I had a lovely view of Cindy's tongue darting in and out of Rachael at an incredible pace. I wondered how she made it move so fast. Rachael was not insensitive to the feelings produced by Cindy's tongue and had a shattering orgasm. Just before she rolled off me, she gave my cunt one last deep kiss. I was spent from my own orgasm, but I still wished that there was a man in the room. I desperately wanted to be fucked right then.

However, I was to have to wait for that pleasure. Cindy moved into position over me and lowered her cunt onto my mouth. I readily began licking her and tried to imitate her rapid movements, but I simply could not make my tongue move that fast. Cindy was giving me the same treatment she gave Rachael, and in a few more minutes I had another orgasm. I hadn't noticed that Rachael had gotten dressed again until Cindy rose from me and I recovered my composure. When I stood up Rachael came over and kissed me on the cheek. As she put one hand on my cunt and slid a finger inside, she told Cindy that I was indeed a rare find. Then she told Cindy to help me get dressed because there were two men due in a few minutes who would love to fuck the two of us. Cindy totally shocked me when she said that I had made a new friend Saturday night who she thought would also like to work here. I hadn't ever thought of Lisa at a place like this, but when I did start thinking about it I thought she might be interested. Rachael told us to bring her around when we were ready, or maybe she could go out on a "date" like I had Friday night. I thought this would be the best way to introduce Lisa to our profession and made up my mind to get in touch with her.

CHAPTER 9
My First Job at Rachael's

Cindy and I went to freshen up as Rachael went to meet the two men who would arrive shortly. When Cindy took me in the bathroom, I just stopped and looked around. I had never seen such a beautiful bathroom, even in the movies. I was almost afraid to use such a beautiful place, especially the towels, but Cindy said not to be silly. What good were things if they weren't used. That made sense, so I finished cleaning up. I especially wanted my cunt to smell fresh if a new man was going to have me. I didn't know how he would feel about the strong smell of sex that I so loved from women's cunts. When we were finished, we both looked at ourselves in the mirror and smiled. Cindy said, "All right, you're gorgeous. Just don't let them tear the clothes off you. Clothes cost too much." Then she kissed me on the cheek. I returned the kiss and squeezed her hand as we left the room.

I hadn't thought I would be so nervous but I was very scared when Rachael asked us to go to the den to meet two gentlemen. The den was where the bar was. Cindy whispered to me to have a strong drink when we got there to calm my nerves.

Rachael introduced us to Roger and Jeff, who were from Seattle. They seemed nice enough and were in their mid-forties. Cindy had never met either one of them either, but Rachael had assured her earlier that they were quite nice. Cindy was very concerned that I should have a good experience my first time at Rachael's. I asked for a scotch and soda when they asked me what I wanted to drink. I still remember Jeff's smile breaking into a chuckle as I jumped a little when one of the ice cubes bumped my nose. He must have realized how nervous I was. The drink did have a calming effect on me, but I didn't want any more when it was offered.

Actually no one took a second drink. Rachael had told Cindy earlier that these two men liked to hire two girls and have both of them in one bedroom. Cindy said she thought we ought to go have some fun and led the way to a bedroom with an enormous bed. Jeff put his arm around me as we followed Cindy and Roger, and I noticed that he could not keep from letting it slip down to my ass. I smiled and told him it felt good, but then I remembered what Rachael had said about anal intercourse and wondered if by rubbing my ass, Jeff was signaling that that was what he wanted. Then I decided that I was just being paranoid, and really began to enjoy the feeling.

As soon as I shut the door, Cindy turned and began to kiss Roger. I immediately did the same with Jeff. I noticed that Jeff's hands were constantly busy and he shortly had my skirt off and his hand inside my panties. He immediately noticed that I was becoming wetter and wetter as he continued playing with me. I was unbuckling his belt and unbuttoning his shirt as he took my jacket off. My blouse quickly followed and he stopped to whistle, saying, "My God, Roger, look at this girl. She's beautiful."

Roger was just taking off Cindy's blouse and said the same about her. Cindy had worn beautiful blue lingerie and was absolutely beautiful with her blond hair, and her face becoming flushed from the activity. Roger replied that we were both beautiful and unhooked Cindy's bra. I now had Jeff's shirt loose and his pants undone. I was kissing his chest while I reached for his cock. He had his hand in my panties again and slipped a finger up my cunt. I was much wetter now and loved the feeling as he moved his finger in a circular motion getting me hotter and hotter. I soon had his cock free from its confinement and dropped to my knees to suck him. He was not unduly large so I had no trouble taking him to the balls in one movement. As I was sucking I heard him ask Roger why wives couldn't suck like this. I thought to myself that it was a good thing that wives were so stupid. Otherwise I wouldn't be able to make money so easily doing something I would have done for free.

I glanced over to Cindy and Roger to see what they were doing. Roger was sitting on the bed with Cindy kneeling in front of him bobbing her head up and down on his cock. As I watched her for a minute I got more excited and worked harder on Jeff. I felt his balls pull up tight and realized he was going to come shortly. I started moving my head faster and faster and squeezed his balls. That did it. He shot off in my mouth and grabbed the back of my head to hold it in place. He needn't have worried. I wouldn't have pulled my mouth away from a coming cock if the house was on fire, but I did kind of like the feeling of force holding me in place as he pumped a lot of cum in me. The sounds of Jeff coming must have spurred Roger on to his finish, because he started moaning as Cindy swallowed all of his cum.

I was rubbing Jeff's cock all over my face as I watched Cindy complete her work on Roger. She shortly got up and went to the bathroom. While she was there, Roger got up and stood next to Jeff. I took his cock and began rubbing it on my face as I was doing with Jeff's. Roger started getting hard again in no time. I didn't know if I was supposed to suck both of them or not, but I assumed I was because both Jim and Harry had fucked both Cindy and me in the mouth as well as the cunt so I didn't see any harm in Roger getting hard. Cindy came back and said I was greedy. She took Jeff's hand and led him to the bed. This time she sat on the bed while Jeff stood in front of her. He got hard again almost as soon a she started sucking him. I guess that men get hard quicker if they have a different girl working on them.

Roger's cock was fully hard by this time and he pulled me up and led me to the bed. When I got to the edge, he gave me a slight push and I took my favorite fall. He looked down on me for a minute and then laid on top of me. I guided his cock to its target and truly enjoyed the feeling of having a new man in me. Cindy had moved in the same position I was in and Jeff followed Roger's lead. Pretty soon the bed was moving with the beautiful tempo of sex. Since both Roger and Jeff had already come once, they lasted a long time. About every five minutes they switched places, so we both got to fuck each man many times. Finally Roger came in my cunt and soon after Jeff came in Cindy. After a few minutes of small talk they each got dressed and left. Thus was my initiation in Rachael's house complete.

Afterwards, Cindy took me to the bathroom and gave me a very pleasurable sponge bath. I promptly returned the favor, taking as much time on her pussy as she had on mine. I realized that it was vital that my cunt always appear fresh when I first met a man, so I wasn't surprised when she told me to always take the time to thoroughly wash myself after each client. No man wanted to smell another man's odor on a girl (unless it was like the two men we just had where they shared us). All of this made perfect sense to me so I had no trouble doing as she said. Besides, it felt good to be clean after so much activity. Even though I had just knelt on the floor and lain on the bed, I tended to move a lot when I was having sex, especially when I was lying on the bed. I have heard a lot of jokes about women, especially wives, who just lie there when a man fucks them and I can't figure out how they do it. Even if I don't come with a man, as I didn't with either Jeff or Roger, I still move a lot when I'm being fucked. It just seems natural and it makes it more enjoyable for me. I love the feeling of a prick rubbing against my cunt walls and the easiest way to ensure that is to move my ass in a circular motion.

I thought we were done for the day, but Cindy told me to get dressed and see if Rachael had anything else for us. We went out to the den to see if anyone was there. The only person there was another girl whose name was Linda. She said hello but didn't seem very friendly at all. Cindy later told me that Linda had a drinking problem and Rachael never let her go out on dates with men because of it. If she worked in the house, Rachael could make sure she didn't have anything to drink. Actually Cindy thought that Rachael was making her go for treatment for alcoholism, but she wasn't sure. My father has a drinking problem. I don't know if you could call him an alcoholic, but his drinking definitely gives my mother a lot of grief. I made up my mind that I was never going to get addicted to anything and told Cindy this. She laughed and said she thought I was already addicted to sex. When I didn't laugh with her right away, she told me to take it easy, she was only kidding. However, I thought there might be more than a grain of truth in what she said. I decided that if I was going to be addicted to something, it may as well be something that paid me instead of something that cost money.

As we were standing around talking, Maria brought a group of men to the den. One of them obviously knew Linda very well, because they immediately kissed and started talking. They left the room after a couple of minutes before I even learned who he was. The other three men were obviously disappointed that there were only two of us there. They thought one of them would have to go without a girl or have seconds. (Men are funny. They don't mind being second, third, or fourth when they're in a group situation, but when it's one at a time, they all want to be the first.) Cindy told them we had just got to the house and were anxious to have a little fun. She said she knew she could easily drive two of them out of their minds if they wanted a little three-way action. The two older men decided to go along with this idea. This left me with a slightly overweight man named Ross who looked like he was in his late thirties.

Ross had obviously been to the house before, because he led me to a bedroom on the third floor which had a beautiful four-poster in it. (As in all beds in Rachael's house, there were no bedspreads or blankets on the bed, only beautiful satin sheets.) He said Rachael had told him that I was new as of today, but she didn't think I would mind being a little kinky. I looked at him warily and he noticed it right away because he told me to relax. He said he just liked to tie girls up when he had sex. I wouldn't be hurt at all. Even the ropes were velvet. I was totally unprepared for this. In fact, I had never even thought of being tied up. I was afraid that he was going to tie me face down and fuck me in the ass, but he didn't do that at all. After spending a few minutes (too few minutes for me), caressing my breasts and legs, he undressed me, but left my stockings and bra on. I was nervous when he got some beautiful red velvet rope from a dresser and began to tie my wrists to the posts at the head of the bed. He was still totally dressed and this seemed to make me feel even more helpless.

When he finished tying my legs to the posts at the foot of the bed I was lying spread-eagled on the bed with my pussy fully exposed. I felt scared but incredibly aroused. I wasn't scared that he would hurt me. I believed Rachael when she had told me that she didn't allow that, but I was scared of the unknown. I could feel my pussy getting wetter and wetter as I was getting more and more aroused. Finally he had me where he wanted me and began to remove his clothes. As I said before he was a little overweight and thus not as appealing as some of the other men I had screwed recently. However, when he was fully naked he gave me a treatment I had never expected. He went to the dresser again and got out a big feather. Now I was scared, because I am very ticklish and I was afraid he was going to torture me with it. Actually he used it in a very sparing and erotic manner. He kissed my body all over as he dragged the feather up one leg and down the other. He didn't let it touch my pussy at all. It was just serving to get me hotter and hotter. Finally, he began to lick my pussy. (I was glad that Cindy had insisted on giving me such a good washing there.) When he licked my pussy, the feather began to graze over my breasts, but it totally missed my nipples. I was beginning to get seriously hot. I wasn't sure if it was more because of him eating my pussy or the treatment on my breasts, but the combination was driving me crazy. After a few minutes my body began to heave right off the bed and I knew I was going to have an orgasm. Just as I started my orgasm, he took the feather from my tits and applied it to my cunt lips. By this time they were super-sensitive and this absolutely drove me nuts. My shoulders and my feet were the only part of my body on the bed as he continued to fuck me with the feather. I swear that my ass was a foot off the bed and would have been even higher if it weren't for the ropes.

As he kept up the pressure on my cunt, I couldn't hold it in any longer and began to scream from the pleasure. Finally he took the feather from my cunt and let me calm down. When I opened my eyes, I saw him smiling at me. He leaned over and kissed my mouth with the tenderest kiss I have ever had. I wanted to put my arms around him and hug him but I couldn't because of the ropes holding my arms. I wasn't in distress over this for very long when he put a pillow under my ass and climbed on top of me. Because of the ropes I couldn't guide him into me, but he seemed very able to do that himself. I had to admit that my cunt was rather loose from all the activity he had put it to, so his cock did slide in rather easily. I could barely feel him on the walls, so I began to rotate my ass.

Now I could feel his cock, and it felt wonderful. I knew I wouldn't have another orgasm but I was enjoying this immensely. He was obviously enjoying it too, because he came quite quickly. When he began to come he pulled out of me and moved up and put his cock in my mouth. I swallowed everything that he pumped in me and was quite proud of myself. He was evidently pleased too, because when he collapsed on top of me, he whispered that I was wonderful, and he couldn't believe this was the first time I had ever been tied up. I assured him it was, and kissed him with true feeling and thanked him for a wonderful time.

After a couple of minutes of resting, he got up and began to loosen the ropes so I could sit up. As soon as I could sit up, I took his cock in my mouth again and cleaned him completely off. He was genuinely surprised at this, so I told him that I had really enjoyed him and wanted him to see me again. He got hard again and seemed very surprised. I was only pleased, and pushed him back on the bed. When he was lying on his back, I mounted his cock and eased it into my cunt. I again started rotating my ass as I moved up and down. He was holding on to my hips and bucking up into me as I kept this us for over ten minutes. Finally I realized he wanted to cum again, but was having trouble. I reached down and massaged his balls for a minute before I stuck my finger up his ass. This sent him off like a rocket and he almost threw me off him with the force of his thrust. I could feel the cum hitting the walls of my cunt as he continued to spurt into me. Finally he calmed down and closed his eyes, but he was still breathing hard. When he opened his eyes, he told me he had never met anyone like me in his life. When he said he wished he weren't married, I began to get a little worried and asked him what he meant. He said he just meant that his wife wouldn't do any of these things and thought he was sick, but I seemed to enjoy them. I told him that it was true that I did enjoy sex. I enjoyed it a lot, but I don't know if I would enjoy being tied up every day. Maybe a little variety was what she needed. As soon as I said this I resolved to myself never to say anything like it again. I was beginning to sound like an advice column. He now got up and dressed to leave. I followed him to the door telling him I had to go to the bathroom before I came back downstairs. As he turned to say goodbye, I gave him another kiss and again asked him to ask for me again. He kissed me back and said, "Thank you." He shut the door and I went to clean myself up before going back downstairs.

When I got back downstairs, I again went back to the den. This time Rachael was the only one there. She looked pleased to see me and told me she had heard good reports about me from all three men. I guess it was her practice to question her steady customers about any new girl she hired. She said they all said they got more than they expected and hoped to see me again. She was truly astounded that Ross had fucked me after untying me. In all the years he had been coming to her house, he had never come twice in one night, and had always had the girl tied up. It was the only way he could come. I had a horrible thought and said, "Suppose he goes back to just sleeping with his wife. You'll lose his business." Rachael smiled and told me not to worry about it. Chances of it were remote and even if he did, he would have nothing but good things to say about us, so we would probably end up with some of his friends. I guess this made sense. I was really surprised at her long-term view of business.

Cindy came down after a few more minutes and asked Rachael if she had any girls coming in for the night. She said we both had work to do for tomorrow and really should be getting back. Rachael told her that was fine; she had plenty of help for the night, so we got ready to leave. She gave us each an envelope when we left, but neither Cindy or I looked in it. We just put them in our purses and said good night. I thought it would have been tacky to look in the envelope in front of Rachael, but I could hardly refrain myself when we got outside. However, Cindy said to wait until we got in a cab to look. There was no object in letting anyone on the street see us with money. As soon as we got in and settled, I couldn't wait any longer. When I finally opened it I was very presently surprised. I was paid $75 for my time with Jeff and Roger. Rachael had listed her fees for each activity. It cost each of them $150 to get both a blow job and fucked by each of us, and this fee was split 50–50 with Rachael and us. Thus she made $150 and we split $150. This seemed fair to me because she had the house to maintain and she was the one with the list of customers. What really surprised me was my payment for Ross. Because he insisted on tying girls up and liked new girls, he had to pay more. He paid $200 just for me, but he was so pleased after

fucking me a second time that he had given Rachael
an extra $100. She passed this entire "tip" on to me.
So I made $100 for being tied up and being fucked
and another $100 for fucking him after he untied
me. I couldn't believe I had earned $275 in less than
three hours this afternoon. I felt great as the cab
pulled up to our lousy hotel. Remembering the food
at school, I told the driver we had changed our
minds and wanted to go to the *Top of the Sixes*. (It
was the only really good restaurant I knew.) Cindy
looked startled for a minute and then laughed at me
and I said, "My treat."

CHAPTER 10
A Boring Weekend

I had a lot of schoolwork to do the rest of the week,
so I didn't go with Cindy on Thursday when she went
over to Rachael's again. I was kind of hoping that
something would come up for the weekend, but
Cindy didn't mention anything about going out when
she got back from Rachael's. She said she was going
to Philadelphia again this weekend, so I realized we
wouldn't be going out. Steve did call Thursday night
and asked me out for Saturday night and I accepted
even though I wasn't crazy about the idea of being
alone with him again. I had been hoping that if any
of the boys from last weekend called me, it would be
Andy.

I had put $220 in the bank of Wednesday, so I
now had a total of $260 safe and sound. This didn't

leave me over $15 after subtracting the cost of the meal with Cindy. I decided I was going to have to watch my spending if I wanted to get out of college with enough money to pay off my student loans. I went to the movies with Kathy on Friday night and then straight to bed.

When Steve showed up on Saturday night, I had no idea what we were going to do. I was very pleased when he said he had tickets to *Fiddler on the Roof.* I had never been to a Broadway show before and I really enjoyed this. Afterward he took me to a Hungarian restaurant where the food was both very good as well as very reasonable. He told me the first thing to learn about New York restaurants is that ethnic food is usually very good and reasonable. However, and most important of all, French food is never truly ethnic, and never inexpensive. (I have found his information to be accurate in almost all cases and really love the wide diversity of restaurants in New York.)

Things were a little awkward near the end of dinner, but he finally asked me if I wanted to go back to his apartment. I asked him if we would be alone and he said he wasn't sure, but he didn't want another scene like last weekend. When I asked him what was the matter with last weekend, he looked shocked and said he couldn't believe I had behaved that way. I told him that if I remembered correctly, he hadn't refused to screw any of the girls that were there. He reddened a little at this and said he still couldn't believe I was that kind of girl, and if I was going to continue screwing his friends, we would have to break up. I said I could quit screwing his friends (although I did want to have Andy again),

81

but what about other people. He might not screw my friends, but I was sure he wasn't going to pass up any other girl that came along.

Besides, I told him, "I really don't mind if you fuck my friends. I brought Cindy over for just that purpose. I was proud of the way you can fuck. You really are a great fuck. I get hot just watching you in action with other women. I was surprised that I didn't feel the least bit jealous as I watched you with Cindy, or even Lisa, who I just met. I was really proud of your ability to render them senseless, but I'm not going to put up with any bullshit like you calling me names and trying to put me down. I'm just as good as you are, and I'm just as free to enjoy life as you are. If I see a gorgeous man and he has some interest in me, he'll probably nail me, and I won't feel used at all. I don't feel cheap or sluttish when I screw someone I just met. I just feel good. If you want a girlfriend who's going to sit home and knit while you're out having a great time, you'll have to search elsewhere."

"Suppose I don't go out? Suppose I remain faithful to you?"

"Forget it. I don't believe you could, and I wouldn't want you to. Besides, didn't you hear me? I liked to be screwed. I like to fuck men, and I can't really see myself being faithful to anyone right now."

I almost said at least until I make a lot more money, but I stopped in time. I didn't mention last Tuesday at Rachael's. I knew he would have thought I was just a cheap slut if he knew I had purposely gone there and screwed men for money. He asked me again if I wanted to go back to his apartment and I told him I thought I would pass on it for tonight. It was all kind of sad when he kissed me good-night back at my dorm. I probably could have sneaked him upstairs past the guard on the floor, but I just didn't feel like it. I just went straight up and off to bed.

Sunday I managed to get a lot of work done for the next week at school. I was hoping Rachael would call or Cindy would come up with something for the week or weekend, and I figured if I was ahead on the work I had to do at school, I could take the time off with no worries about school. When Cindy got back Sunday night, she told me that she was sure something would come up this week. I was curious about her trips to Philadelphia so I asked her if she was from there and went to visit her family. I wasn't at all surprised when she told me that her trips to Philly were always business trips and extremely profitable. Evidently she had met some very wealthy people at a convention there once and had been going back ever since occasionally for what she called "corporate work." When I looked puzzled at this phrase, she explained that a lot of corporations used call girls as the icing on the cake for a business deal. I laughed out loud when she said her title with the company was "marketing consultant"; then I realized that she actually had a position with the company.

"You mean you actually draw a salary from the business and pay taxes and everything?"

"Absolutely. You can only make so much illegal money, you know. This way I have a source of income that's totally legit and I even have a pension plan. And you know what's really nice?"

"What?"

"The company is paying for my college education."

Every day I was learning something new. It had never occurred to me that being a call girl could be considered anything other than a disdainful profession. Now I realized that I was rooming with a girl who was using her expertise at sex to obtain a college degree, build up her assets and generally plan for her future, and the great American corporations were helping her every step of the way. I decided that I had a lot to learn. I also decided that I should make a business plan for myself, both for my college years and afterward.

I was happy to hear from Rachael Monday, but my period was due on Tuesday so I couldn't go over there on Tuesday. But she was very nice about it and suggested that I come over on Saturday afternoon.

CHAPTER 11
All Alone at the House

On Friday Cindy said she couldn't go to Rachael's Saturday afternoon, because she was being sent out with a crazy Englishman for the entire weekend. I had trouble picturing an Englishman as crazy, but she assured me that this one was. She said she should be back by Sunday night and if she wasn't, to call the Marines. I didn't know what to think of that, so I just told her to have a good time. She said she would and to rest up tonight so I would be ready for Saturday.

I studied till midnight Friday and on Saturday morning. I was completely caught up with all of my work when I got dressed to leave for Rachael's. I wore a little blue corset and stockings that I had bought in the Village. It left both my breasts and my pussy bare. Technically it came with skimpy panties, but I didn't bother wearing them. I felt extremely sexy when I finished dressing in a low-cut blouse and mini-skirt with no panties on. In fact I felt positively wicked. I was glad it was a little chilly out so I had an excuse to wear a long coat, because I didn't want the girls I lived with to know how I was dressed for Saturday afternoon.

I was a little early (boy, talk about being eager), so I walked the distance to Rachael's house. It was really a beautiful day in early November and I enjoyed the walk. When I went up the stairs and knocked at the door, I didn't feel like a call girl at all. I just felt like a girl going to visit a good friend. Maria led me to the den as soon as I removed my coat, and told me I was going to have a busy day. It seems that the other two girls who were supposed to be there had called in sick, and Rachael was frantically trying to find someone else to fill in for them. Some of her girls couldn't get away on Saturday because they were married and were spending time with their husbands. I could just imagine being married and telling my husband that my madam had called and I had to go fuck a few guys this afternoon. I told Maria I needed a busy day and was looking forward to it. I think she thought I meant I needed the money, which was true, but I needed the sex too. I hadn't fucked anyone since the last time I was here ten days ago, and I really wanted to fuck.

There were three men in the den waiting for girls

when Maria finally got me there. She introduced them as John, Brian and Charles. She told them I was new here and they had to take it easy on me. After a few minutes of small talk, John said he had been the first one to arrive and so he guessed that made him lucky. He led me to one of the bedrooms on the next floor. As soon as the door was shut, he pulled me in his arms and began to remove my clothing. When my blouse and skirt were gone, he whistled at my lingerie and said, "New, huh? You look like you were made for this job." I replied, "Clothes make the woman," and reached for his cock. He was trying to suck my tits as I was unbuckling his belt, but gave up when I sank to my knees to suck his cock.

He was already hard, but I could easily take him to the hilt in my mouth. I felt his hands on the back of my head as he began to fuck my face. I have noticed that almost all men do this when I am on my knees in front of them. It must give them a sense of power or something, but I never complain because I like it. As long as I don't gag, I have no problem with someone forcing his cock in my throat. I was surprised when I suddenly felt his balls tighten up and the fluid shooting out of him and into my mouth. I hadn't expected him to come so quickly.

He seemed angry that he had come so quickly and said that he hoped I didn't expect to get off that easily. I was ticked at this. I hadn't even gotten up, let alone made any movement like I wanted him to leave. But I was very sweet when I told him that I fully expected to be fucked and was more than willing to help him get hard again. After all, he was the one paying and I was supplying the service. I decided to teach him what service with a smile was. I led him over to the bed and went to work on his soft cock. It wasn't long before he was hard again, but I noticed that he wasn't nearly as hard as before. However, I thought it was hard enough to get in my pussy, so I climbed on top of him and lowered myself on his cock. As I began to pump up and down and rotate slightly, I could feel him getting harder. Finally he was hard enough for me to start moving faster and make him come. After I had kept this up for about ten minutes, I thought I had better speed things up a little, so I put a finger in his ass and rubbed lightly in there. I felt him grow bigger real fast and then he grabbed me and slammed into me filling me with his second load. As his cock shrank and finally slid out of me, he kissed my cheek and said I was terrific. I told him he was pretty good himself and gave his cock a final kiss.

John then got up to get dressed and left. Maria came in and said she would bring Brian up in about ten minutes, if that was enough time for me to get ready. She stopped and looked at me for a minute and asked me where I got my lingerie, and said I looked beautiful. I thanked her and told her where the shop was. I was picturing how she would look in their stuff. I decided she would look real good as she turned to leave. Maria is only about thirty and has an excellent figure. She came back briefly to tell me to greet Brian just in the lingerie. He would love it.

I assumed she knew what she was talking about, so after cleaning up, I didn't bother to put on my skirt and blouse. I decided to wait in the bathroom until I heard the door open and shut and come out just wearing my corset and stockings. When Brian came in I told him I would be out in just a minute. It sounded just like he was picking me up for a date in high school, but when I came out I didn't look like any high school girl I had ever known. I saw the glow in his eyes as I came over to him and put my arms around his neck. I raised my face to his and he kissed me over and over. I heard him say, "My God, you're beautiful," as he kept kissing me and massaging my back. I led him over to the bed and started removing his clothes. I took off his jacket and unbuttoned his shirt. He wasn't very handsome, but he had a beautiful body; lots of muscles and a flat stomach. I kissed his body from his neck to his navel before I even started taking off his pants. I could feel the blood pumping excitedly through the veins in his muscles as I continued removing his clothes. I was becoming very pleased with my ability to make men happy. I could see how a girl could make a lot of money at this, like Cindy and Rachael, if she did it right.

He was soon totally naked in front of me. He had the best body I had ever seen. It wasn't skinny like a lot of younger boys, but the perfectly developed body of a mature man. I suddenly wanted this man very much. I started rubbing his cock all over my face. Even the texture of his cock was perfect. If I had died while rubbing it on my face, I know I would have died happy. However, I soon felt it getting hard, and decided that I should do my job and give him all the pleasure I could. I took his cock in my mouth and worked my way down to the base. I loved the feel and taste as it slid to the back of my throat. He also put his hands on the back of my head and began to fuck my mouth. This was all right with me because I just wanted to do whatever made him happy.

I played with his balls all the while he fucked my mouth, but he never came close to coming. After he tired of my mouth, he gently pushed me back on the bed and turned me over. I thought he was going to fuck me in the ass. I figured Rachael was so short-handed that she hadn't told him that I didn't do that, but he just got on his knees and began to eat me out. I was a little nervous at first because I thought I might have some of John's cum in me even though I had douched. If I did Brian never noticed or said anything. He just proceeded to drive me crazy with his tongue. He used one of my favorite tricks and put a finger up my ass when I was close to coming. This drove me over the edge and I screamed with pleasure as he slowly ceased eating me.

I felt guilty that he had made me come, but had not come himself. I told him that he was the one who was supposed to enjoy himself, not me, and he said that it was impossible for him to enjoy sex if his partner does not have a good time. I told him, "I like the way you think." Then I decided that I had better get down to business and make him as happy as he had made me. He was still hard from fucking my mouth, so he started to fuck me with my face still down on the bed and my ass raised in the air. He slid his prick into me in one stroke and began to fuck me hard, like Steve did. I could feel myself moving across the bed with the force of his thrusts. I must have been getting too far away from him, because he pulled me back to the edge of the bed so he could continue to stand on the floor as he fucked me. It seemed like he was never going to come, when he finally pulled out and turned me over. I guided his cock into me as he climbed on top of me. In this position he fucked much slower than he did standing on the floor. It finally occurred to me that h wasn't going to come until I had another orgasm, so I began to move my ass like I was on the verge of coming. He began to pump faster and faster as I returned each thrust. After a few minutes of this frantic screwing, he gave one last thrust and held still as he unloaded into me. I pretended to have another orgasm and started kissing him all over until he finally rolled off me. I didn't have to fake the hard breathing as I lay next to him on the bed. I must have jumped a foot off the bed when he leaned over to kiss me and took one of my tits in his hand. I was just so incredibly sensitive. I returned the kiss with passion and watched him get dressed, still admiring his body as I lay on the bed. I asked him if he knew he had a beautiful body. He leaned over and kissed me and said it was nothing compared to mine. Then he put a finger in my pussy, pulled it back out and sucked it clean in his mouth. "Just to remember your taste," he said as he turned to leave.

I was still relaxing when Maria came in and told me to hurry up. I had to change rooms for Charles. She said to just come down to the den when I was ready. I didn't know why I had to change rooms until I remembered the four-poster, but then I thought maybe she was just going to change the sheets. They were a total mess after Brian and I had finished with the bed. I could see that no man would want to be brought to a bed like this. I got up and thoroughly cleaned myself again, put on my clothes and brushed my hair. When I studied myself in the mirror, I thought I looked as good as I had when I came in the front door. I went down to the den.

Charles seemed happy to see me, but I was surprised because there were four more men there. Maria hadn't told me anything about anyone else showing up. She was probably afraid I would sneak out the back door or something. When I thought of that I realized that I had no idea where the back door was, so I guess Maria was pretty safe. I wasn't going anywhere. Charles took my arm and led me to a bedroom on the third floor. I thought I was going to be tied up again, but he led me to a different room than Ross had the other night.

Charles was kind of in a hurry as he started undressing me, but that was understandable because he had waited so long. I looked at the clock in the room. It was just after four o'clock and I had looked at my watch when I got to the front door. It had been five to three then, so he had been waiting for over an hour.

This room also had a four-poster in it, but the bed had a ceiling over it. I had never seen anything like this except in the movies. I thought it was beautiful. I soon found out the reason for the ceiling. It had a mirror so we could see ourselves. Charles led me to the bed as he unbuttoned my blouse and unzipped my skirt. When it fell to the floor I stepped out of it like I had done it a thousand times. He pushed me back on the bed and I again took my favorite fall. I spread my legs as I hit the bed in obvious invitation. He immediately climbed aboard and I guided his cock into me. I could watch us in the mirror as he pumped in and out of me. I liked this. I had seen

Cindy and other girls get screwed before, but I had never seen myself in the mirror. After a few thrusts, he pulled out and lay down next to me. I asked him what was wrong. He said nothing was wrong, and he was sorry for screwing me so quickly, but he had been thinking about me all the time he was waiting. Then he kissed me and asked me to suck his cock. He got up and straddled me so that I had a leg on each side of my head. I hadn't realized how big his cock was until then. It was a lot like Harry's from a couple of weeks ago. (Weeks? It seemed like ages ago.) He sunk to his balls in my mouth and seemed surprised that I could take him with no discomfort. I glanced up at the mirror and watched myself as his prick filled my mouth. It was a beautiful sight. I was glad to have something that big again and went to work on him with enthusiasm. It wasn't five minutes before he erupted in me. It came so fast that even though he was well down my throat, I couldn't keep it all in my mouth and some dribbled on my chin. I took a finger and wiped it up and then licked my finger off.

As I licked my finger clean, I watched Charles's eyes. He was staring a my mouth with fascination. When my finger was clean, I took his shrinking cock back in my mouth. It fit very easily now that it wasn't so hard anymore. I was very pleased when I felt him start to get hard again. He rolled over on his back as I kept sucking him. I realized that he probably wanted to watch us in the mirror for awhile and I resolved to give him a great show. I kissed, licked and generally made a full production out of sucking his cock. Finally he seemed to have had enough and asked me to climb on him. I was happy to have his big cock in me again. I seemed tighter than I had been when he first fucked me earlier, and I enjoyed the feeling of his cock splitting my cunt. I had to pump up and down a few times until he got all the way in. When I felt his balls against my ass I stopped moving a few minutes and just savored the feeling of being filled. I guess he was having trouble staying still because he started to buck up into me. I started to rotate my ass and meet his thrusts. He was only in me about five minutes when I felt him ram me hard and come deep up my cunt. I laid down on top of him and kissed him over and over, telling him what a great lover he was. He seemed to like this very much. I thought he seemed like he was in a hurry when he got up right away and he replied that he was. He had to meet his wife at five at Bloomingdale's. I told him to wait a minute. "Can't have you smell like pussy, can't we?" I said, and took his cock in my mouth and cleaned him off. I think he appreciated this more than anything else I had done for him. (Silly me.) After I was done, he stood me up and kissed me three or four times. As he got dressed, he said he hoped to see me again. I truthfully told him I hoped to see him again too.

This time when Maria came up to get me I was ready for her and went downstairs with her. I asked her how many men were downstairs now and she replied that there were only the same four. Two more had come, but they were old customers and Rachael was taking care of them herself. Maria said this was extremely rare. "Only four," I replied. "When was the last time you screwed four men in one day?" I felt a little ashamed when she said never, but then she said she sometimes thought about it, and giggled like a schoolgirl.

She introduced me to the four men I had only met momentarily before. I remember there was someone named Bill, but he didn't look at all like my Bill, and someone else named Gary, but I can't remember the other two names no matter how hard I try. They were evidently all together because Gary said they were in kind of a hurry. I wondered if they had to meet their wives like Charles did. One of the men asked Maria if she had a bed big enough for all four of them at once with me. I looked at him and then at all of the other ones in disbelief. "All at once?" I said. The one who had spoken looked surprised and said, "Why not? You're going to take all of us anyway aren't you. This will just save you getting dressed each time." I kind of shrugged my shoulders and said, "Indeed, why not?" Maria led us to the original room that Cindy and I had used the first night I was here. It had a huge bed.

When we all got in the room, one of the men said, "Why don't you do a little striptease?" I was clearly flustered because I had no idea how to do a striptease. The only places I had ever known of girls doing such things were at county fairs and I had never seen them perform. One of the other men told him to take it easy, Maria had said I was new. I made up my mind to give Maria a tip later that night when I got paid.

None of the men seemed really disappointed that I was so inexperienced. One of them even remarked that I looked like one of his daughter's friends. One of the others immediately said that he probably wanted to fuck her too. The first one said he couldn't deny that and started to take off my blouse. I breathed a sigh of relief. Now I was back on familiar territory. Another man unzipped my skirt. Two of them whistled as I stepped out of my skirt and tossed my blouse aside. I heard a lot of compliments.

"She is beautiful."

"I'll bet your daughter's friend doesn't wear lingerie like that."

"I don't know, but my daughter better not."

Much as I loved the compliments, I decided that I had better get things moving. I knew it would take me awhile to take care of them all. I asked them what they would like to do first. One decided that I should suck his cock first and started getting undressed. Everyone else followed suit. Pretty soon I had four naked men in front of me. I dropped to my knees and started sucking on their cocks one at a time. Two of the men moved kind of close together and I managed to get both of their cocks in my mouth at once. There was something about this scene that just seemed to drive everyone to higher and higher heights of sensuality. When I didn't have a man's cock in my mouth or hand, they were stroking themselves. This seemed to continue for quite awhile. My knees were getting sore when one of the guys finally came. I grabbed his cock and put it in my mouth as he started coming on my face. I managed to swallow most of his cum. This was the trigger that set off the rest of the group. Before I knew what was happening, my face was being bombarded with cum. I was moving my head from one cock to another to try to get it in my mouth as it erupted. I failed miserably and ended up with semen all over my face and in my hair.

My breathing was still heavy as they finished shooting all over me. I looked up at them, but only one had his eyes open. This was Bill. He was almost as nice as my Bill. I saw his lips make the words, "You're beautiful." I wasn't too sure about that right then. I felt kind of wasted, but then two of the men helped me to my feet and led me to the bed. I realized that I was going to be fucked by all four now. Cindy had once told me that being gang-banged at a party was what had convinced her to start selling her pussy. I knew that I was going to be gang-banged and there was nothing I could do about it, because I had agreed when I came to the room with these four men.

It wasn't as bad as I had feared it would be. Bill was the first to take me. He was still hard, so when I lay on the bed he got on me and spread my cunt with his fingers. When he had me opened up, he rammed his cock in with one push. I was glad he wasn't as big as Charles had been. It went in with no problem. One of the other men crawled on the bed and put his cock next to my face. Another one shortly did the same. I alternated from one cock to the other. This left Gary with no place for his cock. He started sucking my tits and running his hands all over my chest. I reached down and grabbed his cock with my hand and started playing with it and his balls. I didn't want him to feel as if I were ignoring him. I was also beginning to seriously enjoy myself. After a few minutes of this, they all switched places. Bill moved up to my mouth, Gary to my cunt, and one of the other men started playing with my breasts as I played with his cock. Every few minutes they kept moving around. It was kind of like playing a sexual musical chairs.

However, even though I liked this at first, I shortly grew tired of it because I just had too much to do, and I wasn't doing anything very well. As you know I like to move with the men who are fucking me and now I was just kind of lying there. Evidently the men were coming to the same conclusion. Suddenly two of them decided to take a break and just watch for awhile. When they left, the other two moved me around. I was placed on my hands and knees. One of the guys sat near my mouth and I eagerly started sucking his cock. Gary got behind and started fucking me from the rear, not in the rear, just doggie style. I like this position, especially if there are two men, because it allows me to concentrate on what I am doing. I was now able to bring the two men to orgasm rather quickly. Gary started to come in my cunt after only a few minutes and this seemed to spur me on to new efforts with the cock in my mouth. He erupted a couple of minutes later while I could still feel Gary's cock as it began to shrink in me. I swallowed every drop that went in my mouth, thus partially making up for my poor showing earlier.

These two men were immediately replaced by Bill and the fourth man. Bill stuck his cock in my cunt for just a couple of minutes before he came up to the bed and I took him in my mouth. I could taste my juices as well as Gary's cum on his cock. This just seemed to excite me all the more as the last guy entered my cunt.

As I sucked Bill I could hear them all talking. The guy in my cunt said, "This girl's amazing. She was born to fuck. It feels like her pussy is kissing my cock. I've never felt anything like it before in my life."

Bill said, "Let's not forget what a great cocksucker she is. I can feel her tongue all along my shaft. Oh God, if only all women could do this. Ooohl!"

The last word was because Bill had suddenly started to come. His cum hit my mouth so hard that I took his cock out of my mouth. The second shot went at least four feet into the air and came down on my back. The third went up at least two feet. I quickly put his cock back into my mouth and swallowed the last six spurts. Of course they constantly diminished in force. I had never really thought about how much energy men expended in sex before, but now I was truly impressed. As soon as Bill had started coming, the guy in my cunt began to pump me harder and harder. He started coming just as I was swallowing the last of Bill's load. It didn't feel like he came nearly as hard as Bill, but I couldn't be sure. I knew I was exhausted. I just lay face down on the bed as he slid out of my cunt. I was aware that my ass was sticking up very prominently and if one of them had wanted to fuck it, I wouldn't have had the strength to resist.

I had nothing to worry about in this case. They all decided that it was time they left and started getting dressed. I was beginning to think I was right when I had suspected that they had to go meet their wives. I wondered if their wives wondered how they had spent their afternoon. While I was resting thinking of this, Maria came into the room. I was not happy to see her because I really needed a little rest. I shouldn't have prejudged her so quickly. She told me to take my time getting cleaned up. As soon as she said this she said it looked like I had had a rough time. I told her I could use a little rest, but she told me to get ready and come down for something to eat. I hadn't even thought of food, but now that she mentioned it, it sounded like a great idea.

I dragged myself out of bed and went to the bathroom. God, I was a mess. I hadn't realized I looked as tired as I felt. It took me a good twenty minutes to make myself presentable. In the last four hours I had sucked and fucked seven men. I was wondering how much money I was going to make. When I was with the men, I didn't have time to think about this much, but now I realized I didn't know what Rachael charged for just one man who wanted to fuck me. The first night the guys had wanted two girls and she had charged $150 each, and Ross had been into tying people up (bondage, Cindy called it), but none of these guys tonight had really wanted anything special. The last four would have probably preferred to fuck me one at a time. They probably figured they deserved a discount. Oh well. I would just have to see what I got paid.

When I went downstairs it dawned on me that I had no idea where to go to get something to eat. This wasn't a real problem because I could smell the food. Whatever it was smelled good. I followed my nose to the kitchen and found Rachael there with Maria. Maria had made some baked chicken which was delicious, but Rachael warned me that there were no sauces to put on it because we had to be careful what we ate when we were working. Bad breath would destroy a relationship with a client faster than poor sex. I still thought the food was excellent and told them so. Maria thanked me and started to tell Rachael that she should be proud of me. She said the last four men had come downstairs and told her to keep track of me because they wanted to see me again. I immediately said, "Not all at once again, I hope." Both Rachael and Maria laughed at this and seemed to think it hilarious. Then Rachael said she had charged them an extra $50 each because they had gang-banged me, and her girls were not in the habit of being gang-banged like that. I told her I thought they had probably wanted a discount and they both laughed again and asked why.

I told them that I didn't think I had done as good a job on them a I would have if I had them separately. Rachael kind of sighed and said, "Sharon, honey, you have a lot to learn about men. They had a great time. Men like to put women in a subordinate position, and having you to screw any way they wanted was great for them. I probably didn't charge them enough. You know, the only thing that would have made it better for them is if you were married."

"Married, why would that make it better for them?"

"Because fucking another man's wife is what men like to do most in the world. You're so young and pretty, no, beautiful, that they all want you when they first see you, but some of them must think about their daughters when they look at you."

"I think you're right. One of the men said I looked like one of his daughter's friends, and then later he said that his daughter had better not have lingerie like I had. It must have bothered him a little. I suppose he thinks his daughter might be doing the same things, although probably only with one boy and not groups of guys."

"Don't be too sure of that. There's a lot more group sex going on than anyone knows about. Most of it is threesomes, two guys and a girl or two girls and a guy. Needless to say, I prefer two guys and one girl myself."

"I have to agree with that."

Rachael suddenly changed the conversation and asked me if I had to leave early tonight. I told her I had planned to be back by now, but I could always phone and have one of the girls sign me out for the night if Rachael needed me. She was pleased to hear this. She asked me if Maria had told me about being shorthanded. I said she had said that two girls had not shown up. Rachael said they were definitely sick. She could hear it in their voices when they called. She was sorry I had had to work so hard, but it was definitely appreciated. Because I had helped her when she needed it, she said I could sometimes have my pick of assignment. I must have looked as puzzled as I felt, because she explained that there were often two men who needed a girl at the same time, maybe for a date like my first night, or someone who wanted something kinky. I would sometimes be able to pick which one I wanted.

I suddenly remembered Lisa and said that I would like to go out with Jim and Harry some night and take Lisa if Cindy didn't mind. I was pretty sure Lisa would be glad to go out with the full expectation of being fucked. I just wasn't sure how she would feel about being paid for it, so I would surprise her after the act, just as Cindy had done with me. Rachael said she thought this would be a good idea. She certainly could have used Lisa here tonight. I had to agree with that. The doorbell rang and Maria came back to tell us that Bruce was here right on time. Rachael told me to use the bathroom just off the kitchen to freshen up. I was glad to see there was a toothbrush in a case with my name on it. This woman thought of everything.

Maria came back to get me after she had taken Bruce upstairs to a new room. I told her I had to make a phone call. I called Kathy and told her to sign me out for the night. I think she thinks I'm going to suffer in Hell forever for my sins, but she still seems to like me a lot. Maria told me I was right in thinking the reason for some of the room changes was to give her a chance to change the sheets. I was curious and asked her what time she went home and was very surprised when she said she lived here. That had never occurred to me, but it did make a lot of sense. Just before we got to the hallway where he was waiting, she took me aside and told me I was going to get a workout. I couldn't imagine what would be more of a workout than the last four guys and said so. Maria shook her head and said that wasn't what she meant. Then she took her hands and held them about a foot apart in front of her. I didn't understand her at first, but then it dawned on me she meant his cock was huge. I kind of swallowed and asked her if it hurt. She said it would at first, but I would get used to it. This was the first clue I had that Maria ever slept with anyone. I took a deep breath and went into the room.

I was kind of surprised at Bruce when I first saw

him. He must have been in his late fifties, but he was in very good shape. If his hair weren't gray, he would easily have passed for thirty. He came over to meet me and introduced himself, and said that Maria had told him that she had a surprise for him. Then he smiled and said he was very happy with the surprise. I thanked him and told him I was glad to meet him. Then he said he had a surprise for me. I thought he was talking about his cock, but he didn't mean that at all. He said Rachel had agreed with his request to spend the entire night with me. He said we might go out later to get a late supper. He could see that I was pleased and was not acting when I told him that I would love that. Then he said maybe we could have a little fun first. I agreed that would be a good idea, and to be truthful, my curiosity about his cock was getting the best of me.

Bruce led me to the bed and slowly began to undress me. He highly approved of my corset and stockings. I was very surprised when he turned me on my stomach and began to remove the corset. He said he was going to give me a massage and I should be nude for it. He was already treating my body to lovely sensations as he manipulated the fastenings on the garters holding up my stockings and then rolled them down my legs. This man was an expert. I wondered how many women had enjoyed this treatment. After very carefully laying my stockings on a chair he removed the corset. I was totally naked on the bed. He then proceeded to give me an absolutely exquisite body massage. By the time he was finished, I was totally refreshed and ready for anything he had to offer. He had massaged my back, sides and legs, but had not touched my breasts or pussy. So even though

I was refreshed, I was also totally excited. My pussy was pulsing and my breasts were heaving. I reached for him to take off his clothes.

His body was beautiful. It looked like it had been chiseled out of granite. His stomach was flat and muscled and his ass was tight. His arms were muscular. I was thinking how wonderful it would feel as he held me. However, I hadn't yet seen his cock. He had a jock strap on that hid his cock from my view. Finally, when he realized I was staring right at the huge bulge in the jock strap, he removed it in one quick movement. I actually gasped with shock and amazement. Maria had been totally right about the length of this monster, but she hadn't mentioned the thickness. He was over twelve inches long and thicker than a soda can. I had never imagined such beauty existed. I just lay there gazing at it. I greedily took it in my hands and began to massage it. It was as big as my forearm. When I realized this, I began to have doubts about it going into me.

He saw the hesitation in my face and set about to relax me. He again massaged my neck and back. But this time as he felt me getting warmer he turned me over and began to rub my breasts. The nipples were already hard so he knew I was excited but he still worked them over like he was just starting on me. Finally he turned me over again and moved to my legs, again avoiding my pussy. He very carefully worked on my thighs and ass for what seemed like eternity as I continued to get hotter and hotter. When he turned me over again, I was ready for him to fuck me. I spread my legs to make room for him, but he surprised me again. He pulled me to the edge of the bed and knelt between my legs and began to eat me. My pussy was so hot and wet that I came almost immediately. I knew my juices were soaking his face, but I didn't want him to stop at all. When I quieted down he moved me back toward the center of the bed. Now I knew I was going to be fucked.

I kept my legs spread wide so that he had as easy access as possible. He put a pillow under my ass so that he had a clearer shot at his target. I was still a little afraid, but I was even more excited. I knew there was going to be some pain, but I was sure I could stand it. As he got between my legs, I took his prick in my hand to guide it in me. I couldn't get my hand around the shaft. He was just too big around. I wondered if he had ever had a woman suck his entire cock. I resolved to try after he had finished fucking me (if I were still alive, that is). He told me to let him know when it began to hurt a lot, because he wanted me to enjoy this, not be hurt by it. I remembered how Jack and Harry had just touched my cervix with their cocks and again wondered about my ability to take one that was easily half again as long as theirs.

His head was at my entrance and I could feel my cunt begin to open for him. However it only began to open. Nothing like this had ever been in me before. Steve's cock was big, but nothing like this man's. I asked him to kiss me and he did. It seemed to help a little because I relaxed a little more. The head slipped in. My cunt lips were stretched wide open. He pulled out a little and then pushed in a little farther. When he pushed down, I pushed up. He went in farther. I looked down to watch him for a minute. There couldn't have been any more than three inches in me. For the first time I had real serious doubts about my ability to take the full foot. Bruce noticed me watching and gave a huge shove. It went in another three inches. "Well," I thought, "I'm halfway there." Every nerve in my pussy was tingling. I could feel every vein in his cock as he strove to enlarge me even more. With another shove he reached my cervix. This was like a wall to him. He didn't try to force the issue right away. He just kind of lay together as my cunt got used to his immense size. I could feel the pulsing of his cock inside of me and wondered if he was going to come right away. I needn't have worried.

After a few minutes of rest, he pulled almost all of the way out of me. I started to say, "No, don't go," but then he went back in as far as he had just been. It went much easier this time. He began to increase his tempo as he pumped me. I was getting very hot and was meeting his downward thrusts with everything I had. My body was slamming into his as I bucked upward to meet him. I longed to feel his huge balls slap against my ass as his prick went into me. We kept fucking like this until our bodies were soaked with sweat. Suddenly, I felt an orgasm building and said, "Yes, yes." He must have thought I meant I was ready for the final push, because just as I began to scream from the orgasm, he gave the greatest shove I had ever felt and tore through the last barrier. The intense pleasure of the orgasm was combined with the incredible pain of his cock going up into my womb. I added a second scream and collapsed.

Unfortunately, Bruce was in no mood to stop. He was delirious with lust and kept pumping in and out of me, even though I was doing little more than lying there trying to regain my breath. He would pull almost all the way out and then again slam into me with incredible force, each time going past my cervix. Finally the barrier was no longer a hindrance and he could just pump the full twelve inches in and out of me with no special effort. I finally began to revive and participate. I couldn't believe the incredible sensations as I felt the incredible force of his fucking take total control of me. It seemed like every sensation in my body was dead except for the feeling of his huge cock pumping in and out of me. I wrapped my legs around his waist and returned his thrusts so that his balls were slapping against me and he hit bottom. I was wishing we were in the bed with the mirrored ceiling so I could watch his cock go into me. I wondered if it looked as magnificent as it felt, and magnificent was the only way to describe the feeling. I was again building toward an orgasm as he continued to fuck me. I put my hands on his ass and pulled him in as deep as he could get as I again started to come. This time he came along with me. He gave one last heave that was so strong that my head actually hit the headboard, and then he froze deep inside me. At first I was confused because I could feel his cock throbbing, but I couldn't feel the sperm in my cunt, then it occurred to me that he was coming far past the lining of my cunt walls. He was inside my uterus and I simply couldn't feel the splash of his cum there.

After three orgasms with Bruce, I was in desperate need of rest, but I still hated the thought of his cock shrinking and slipping out of me. I kept my arms around him and kissed his neck and chest as he lay on top of me after he finished coming. I could feel his cock shrinking as he regained his breath. Finally he got up off me and his cock slid out of me. When I looked at it, I saw blood on it. The first thing I thought of was that my period had started out of time, but then I realized that it was blood from the incredible violence of his cock in my cunt. He was immediately apologetic and was definitely concerned about me. I think he was afraid he had seriously injured me. (Later I found out that the only other women who had bled the first time he fucked them were his wife and one other woman.) I told him I was sore, which was true enough, but hoped he had enjoyed himself. He bent down and kissed me, telling me that indeed he had and hoped to do so again later tonight. At the time I didn't know if I wanted to be fucked again that night or not, but I told him I was looking forward to it.

After we rested for a few minutes, I took a tissue and wiped the blood off his cock; then I asked him if he would like to have me again right now or after we went out for dinner. He smiled and said that we should probably go out for dinner. Besides, we had all the rest of the night and tomorrow morning for making love. I had to agree with this, but in truth I hated to leave the bed that I shared with him. I moved down so I could lick his cock and fondle his balls. As I licked the head of his cock, he began to get hard again and warned me that if I kept that up, we would have to wait for dinner. I kept licking and finally took him into my mouth. It was all I could do to stuff the head in my mouth. I really couldn't give it the treatment that I did for other men. Men seemed to love it when I licked their cocks as my mouth slid down to their balls. There was no way I was ever going to be able to do this for Bruce. He was just too big.

He was now hard again. I was surprised he had recovered so fast and I think he was too. He certainly seemed surprised, but he wasn't in any hurry to fuck me again as I thought he would be. He grabbed hold of his cock and began to stroke it while it was still in my mouth. I realized that he wanted to come in my mouth and set out to help him. I kept fondling his balls as I worked as much of his cock into my mouth as I could. I couldn't get it in as far as other men who were not so thick. I had had no trouble taking Jack or Harry to the balls, and they had eight inches, but there was no way I could get more than half of his monster into my mouth. Actually, I don't think I even had that much, but my mouth was stretched to the breaking point. It was probably just as well because Bruce was no stroking himself faster and faster. I began to get rougher and rougher with his balls. Finally I put a finger up his ass and he exploded in my mouth. I was expecting a huge load of cum, probably because of the size of his equipment, but he didn't come much at all. I had no trouble taking every drop down my throat. As his cock began to shrink again, I was able to stuff a little more in my mouth. This seemed to please him enormously. When he had ultimately shrank to what was a normal size for him, I let him slip out of my mouth. I lay next to him on the bed and kissed his chest and face. He reached over to me and pulled me closer, and then just held me without saying a word. He told me that no one had ever done that for him before unless he paid extra for it. When he asked me if I liked it, I told him that I was only sorry that I couldn't give him the same treatment that my boyfriend got. When I saw the look of puzzlement on his face, I told him that I loved the feeling of swallowing a man completely, and I knew that men liked it too, but he was just too big.

Bruce seemed to be interested in my boyfriend. He said it hadn't occurred to him that I had a boyfriend. Then he wanted to know if my boyfriend knew that I worked here. I told him no, but I was thinking of telling him. After all, he had encouraged me to get a lot of experience while I was in school, and I was certainly getting more here than anywhere else. I thought about my use of the phrase "getting more" and giggled. I had to explain the giggle to Bruce and we both had a good laugh over it. I leaned over and kissed his cock again and told him that he certainly had "more" than I had ever expected to find. Once again he kissed me and then decided we should go out for a late dinner.

CHAPTER 12
Dinner with Bruce

After dressing we went downstairs and told Maria we were going out for awhile. She didn't seem to think it was strange for us to be leaving, so I thought Bruce must do this quite often with his "dates." I was glad I had worn my raincoat because it was considerably colder than it had been when I got to Rachael's. With my short skirt and no panties, I would have literally frozen my ass off.

110

I didn't see any name outside the building when we got to the restaurant. Bruce explained that it was actually a private club, and thus not open to the public. (I later found out that members were not allowed to bring their wives. Even single men could not bring girlfriends. It was only for mistresses and call girls.) Inside it seemed like any other nice restaurant. A hostess appeared and showed us to a booth in the back. I had a glass of red wine and was rather surprised when Bruce's "usual" turned out to be straight grapefruit juice. He saw the surprise on my face and explained that he was not a good drinker and simply didn't care for alcohol anymore. I wished my dad felt like this.

We hadn't been sitting there very long when a couple of men stopped by to say hello. Bruce introduced me to each of them, but I can no longer remember their names. They seemed nice enough, but I guess I wasn't really interested in meeting anyone new right then. After all, I had met and screwed eight new men that night. I do remember them asking Bruce when he had met me. When he said, "Tonight," they seemed very surprised. They both looked right at me as if they were judging me in a contest. As soon as they left I asked Bruce what all that was about. He said that it was considered very poor taste to bring someone here whom a man hadn't known for a long time. I naturally asked him why he had brought me the first night. (As soon as I said that, I realized that I was hoping there would be more nights, many more.) I was really curious as to why he would do something that would make other men look down on him. He explained that they wouldn't really look down on him. They were just wondering about me, and he had brought me because he was sure he would see more of me in the future, at least as long as I worked for Rachael. The two guys had naturally noticed that I was pretty, but all of the women in here were.

I took a look around and had to agree with him. I had never seen so many attractive women in one place in my life. Some were absolute knockouts. I would have given anything to have legs like the woman two tables away from us. She was older than I was, and had on a longer skirt, but the skirt had a slit up the side and everyone could see almost to her hip. I decided that she must be a dancer, because her legs were perfect, absolutely perfect. It also occurred to me that these women were probably all very good at what they did. I mean at fucking. If a man didn't normally bring someone here until he had known her for a long time, there must be a reason why they stayed with them for such a long while. After all, none of these couples were married. I suddenly wondered if any of the women were married. I knew they weren't married to the man they were with here, but I remembered Rachael saying that some of the women who worked for her were married. I asked Bruce about this.

He told me that sometimes a man brought in a married woman he was having an affair with, but it was frowned upon if the members knew she was married. The reason was obvious. Once a man had come in with his mistress and found his wife here with a total stranger (to him that is, not to his wife). That was not a pleasant evening for the club members who were present. Bruce had not been at the club that night, but he did know the people involved. He shook his head and said, "Messy situation, very messy."

Our waitress came back to take our orders. I decided to have a steak. I hadn't had a great meal since I took Cindy out the day I first met Rachael (and three nice men). We talked a little more while we were waiting for our food. I kept noticing Bruce staring at me and finally asked him why. He apologized and said it was only because I was so beautiful. I still don't think of myself as beautiful. I know I'm pretty, but I don't think I'm beautiful. However, I never argue with anyone if they call me beautiful. I just say thank you and feel warm inside. I also noticed the two guys who had stopped at our table staring at me a couple of times. Bruce noticed me glance at them and said they were only admiring me, and probably wanted to fuck me. No, they definitely wanted to fuck me and were probably mad at him for getting me first. I asked him if that was part of belonging to the club. Did he have to share any woman he brought in with the rest of the members? He said no, the club had over 500 members, so most women wouldn't agree to being shared by that many people.

When I didn't immediately agree with him, he asked me if I was considering it. I told him that I didn't mind small groups, but 500 did seem a bit much. He then asked me about the "small groups." He commented that some of the members did sometimes have small orgies in the upstairs rooms, and even sometimes took some girls sailing on a yacht. I thought this sounded like a great idea and said so. Then I asked him why the two guys would be mad he had found me first. He took a deep breath and said that it was because of his cock. He was so big that a woman was never as tight after he fucked them as before, and when he was at parties, all the women wanted to try him. I told him I could understand that. As soon as I saw his cock, my mind tended to ignore everything else and become obsessed with getting him hard and in me. He smiled and said, "Thank you. I noticed that you were in kind of a hurry. But if someone else had fucked you as soon as I finished, he would have barely felt you. A day later you would be back almost to normal, but you will never be as tight as you were before tonight." I wondered if Bill would notice when I saw him at Thanksgiving.

Our meals came and we spent the next hour enjoying a terrific dinner. The food here was even better than at the *Top of the Sixes*. When we finally finished eating, we left to go back to Rachael's. I hadn't put my coat on before we went outside. As Bruce held it for me, the wind suddenly blew my skirt up and two boys walking down the street stopped and stared at my bare pussy. One of them called Bruce "Pops" and asked him if he needed any help with his daughter. I told the kid to beat it. Then I nodded at Bruce and said, "He's got more than the two of you put together, and now I'm going to go enjoy it." Bruce seemed amused by the whole thing, but I was ticked off. I thought it might make him mad that they had called me his daughter. He pointed out that he was almost old enough to be my grandfather. This made me feel a little strange, but then I told him that any little girl who thought about her grandfather the way I thought about him would probably be locked up. He laughed and gave me a hard kiss, right out on the street. Then we hailed a cab and started off to Rachael's. As soon as the cab started moving, I leaned over and began to kiss him, just like a schoolgirl. I also began to fondle his cock. When it began to get hard, I unzipped his pants and took him into my mouth. I heard him tell the driver to go for a ride through the park instead of going straight to the address. I felt the cab stop and looked up wondering what had happened, but it was just a red light. When I looked up I saw an old man and woman looking directly at me with their eyes wide open. I must have looked like a scene from a pornographic movie as I had my head in Bruce's lap with part of his massive cock in my mouth. They were still looking as the cab started to move. I pulled my mouth off the cock and licked my lips as I looked directly at the old lady. I thought she was going to have a heart attack. Then I went back to work on Bruce's cock as he started to laugh and we went into Central Park. This time I seemed to be able to take more of his cock into my mouth than I had in the bedroom. I don't know why, but I know it went at least half of the length in, and I think quite a bit more. I felt the huge head going into my throat and thought I was going to choke, but I didn't. Before we were halfway around the park, I had brought him to another orgasm and swallowed ever drop he gave me. I again licked my lips, this time making sure I didn't miss any of his cum. I wanted him all inside of me. I seemed to feel that I have more power if I swallow every bit of a man's cum. I don't know if this is true or not, but I do feel that way. After he came I tucked his prick back into his pants, kissing it just before I put it away, and zipped him up. He pulled me up and put his arm around me, holding me close. When he bent down and kissed me, I felt like I was falling in love again.

I was not comfortable with the thought of being so attached to a customer of Rachael's, but I couldn't really help my feelings. Steve had treated me like a slut, and I was supposed to be his girlfriend. Bruce treated me like a lover and I was only his whore for the night. Actually, I knew I was more to him than a one-night whore, but he did meet me in a whorehouse. He knew I spent my time fucking lots of men there, and I had told him that I didn't mind small orgies, but this didn't seem to matter to him at all. He really seemed to like me. I snuggled up even closer to him just as the cab came out of the park. I was sorry to see the ride coming to an end, but it seemed like we got to Rachael's in just a couple of minutes. I was pleased to see that Bruce was a good tipper. The ride came to $4.85 and he gave the driver $10. We had to wait a couple of minutes for Maria to open the door, but as soon as we were inside Maria led us to Rachael's study. This was the room where I had first met Rachael. When we walked in there was a fire in the fireplace and Rachael was reading. She rose up to greet us and kissed both Bruce and me on the cheek. I was beginning to feel like she was my mother waiting up for me to get home from a date. When she said she wanted to know all about our night together, I started to laugh. She looked at me rather crossly, so I told her that I was sorry but the entire scene reminded me of my mother asking me if I had had a good time. She and Bruce both laughed at this, and Bruce agreed with Rachael that I probably never told my mother anything like Rachael was going to hear.

Bruce started out with a full report on our activities for the entire night. I was a little startled at this, but then Rachael explained that Bruce was an old and very valued customer whom she often asked for reports on her girls. "You mean like a spy?" I said before thinking. Rachael said that companies thought of it as feedback. It was in her best interests to know if her girls were treating the men right. She knew I had already done well because he had taken me out to dinner. This was not something that always happened, and when Bruce mentioned that he had taken me to his "club," Rachael was even more surprised. I was pleased to hear this, but I was truly proud of how Bruce praised me for my efforts to make him happy. Rachael was surprised when he told her about the blow job in bed before we left, and was astounded after hearing about the cab ride. He had never come three times with one girl in one night before, at least not since she had known him.

Later, when Bruce finished his "report," Rachael told me she was very pleased with me. She also said that one of the reasons she had asked Bruce to have me for the night was so that I would have the confidence of knowing that I could fuck any man I ever met, regardless of his size. A few years ago Rachael had lost some business because two of her girls refused to let a man fuck them because of the size of his cock. I guess she could see that this made no sense to me, so she explained that a lot of women are afraid of being hurt by someone like Bruce. She said if the man was rough and the girl not ready, it could cause a lot of pain. Not all men were as nice as

117

Bruce, but almost none had equipment like his. Now that I had been properly broken in, she would feel comfortable sending me out with anyone. She knew I could handle any man's prick without fear. I mentioned that it had hurt a lot when he first went all the way in me, and I was curious to find out if it would hurt so much the second time. Bruce said that I was insatiable, but I was going to have to wait for morning to find out. There was just no way he was going to be able to do anything in bed tonight except sleep, and that was just what he wanted to do, so he and I went up to the bedroom where he had first fucked me.

As soon as we lay down, I felt extremely tired. I suppose this was only natural with all of the activity I had had tonight, but I was surprised at how tired I was. I rolled over against Bruce to kiss him good night. He kissed me back and I laid my head on his chest. I also reached down and caressed his cock and balls. I told him I wasn't trying to start anything, but I just loved handling them. He whispered that was fine with him because he really did want to go to sleep. He did, however, promise to make love to me in the morning. We went to sleep minutes later.

CHAPTER 13
Sunday Morning

I woke up as the sun streamed through the bedroom windows Sunday morning. My hand was still on Bruce's cock and my head on his chest. I must have lain perfectly still all night. I remember thinking that my mom was probably getting ready to go to church, but what I was thinking about wasn't mentioned at church. I was wondering if Bruce was going to make love to me before breakfast or after. I got up and went to the bathroom to clean up. As I was brushing my teeth, Bruce came up behind me and kissed my neck. We were both naked and I could feel his soft cock against my ass as he continued to kiss my neck and shoulders. I finished brushing and turned to return his kisses. I kissed his chest and was working my way down to his cock when he asked me to go to the bed and wait for him.

When he got to the bed, I immediately started to kiss him again. He smelled like he had just come out of the shower, so I knew he had washed all over. I worked my way down to his prick which was still soft. God, even when it was soft it was at least eight inches long and real thick. My hand just reached around it. I resolved to get as much in my mouth as I could before he got hard again. I heard him sigh as my lips went over the head and began to work their way down the shaft. This time he didn't seem as big as he did the night before after he had fucked me. I was making good progress and then he got hard. As soon as he got hard I lost some of the progress I had made and could only keep the head in my mouth. My hand would no longer reach around the shaft. I decided it was time to put his cock where it could fully get into me.

I sat up in bed and straddled him. I knew he could get a little deeper into me this way, which certainly wasn't necessary, but I would have more control over the pace of his entrance. When I looked at it fully hard, I wondered how I had taken it all last night. It still looked frightening to me, but I knew I could do it. I was glad that I had screwed the other guys first last night. That must have opened me up a little bit, and made things easier. However, this was a new day and I was fresh after sleeping so soundly. I lowered myself so that the head brushed my pussy lips. My pussy was soaked with anticipation and desire so there was little resistance for entry. A little push on my part and the head was completely inside me. I stopped for a minute and let my body get used to this invasion. As my cunt muscles relaxed, I pushed down some more and he went in a long way. The end of his prick was up against my cervix again, so I stopped and leaned over to kiss Bruce. He kissed me back and told me to take my time. There was no rush. I felt wonderful as his monstrous prick completely filled my cunt. I think I must have stayed this way for at least five minutes before I worked up the nerve to get the rest of him into me. I began to move up and down with a steady pace. Every nerve in my lower body was afire with passion. I began to feel an orgasm coming on, so I decided that it was now or never and pushed down harder. There was momentary resistance as he hit my cervix again, and then I felt him go through and all resistance disappear. As soon as he went completely into me, I relaxed and this seemed to trigger an enormous orgasm. My entire body felt like it was detached from my mind and was just a center for pleasure. I froze and leaned backward so my back was arched just like it is when I'm lying on the bed and I have a terrific orgasm. Bruce pushed as far into me as possible and held onto my back so I wouldn't fall over. When I calmed down, I totally relaxed and collapsed on top of him.

After a few minutes, Bruce said he hated to tell me this but he was not finished yet. He then rolled me over and began to fuck me with those long strokes. It felt like I was being turned inside out as he pumped me with increasing violence. Every stroke went completely inside, but I felt no exceptional pain. Finally he began to pound into me with incredible force and then he froze with his prick deep inside my cunt. I couldn't feel the sperm but I could definitely feel his balls tighten up against me and I could feel his prick throbbing as he pumped his entire load into me. Now it was his turn to collapse on top of me. We were both completely exhausted, but I felt wonderful. I could hear a church bell ringing and I wondered if my mother had ever felt this wonderful. I couldn't believe that she had. I don't know why unless it was just that I felt so unique and special right then. It seemed impossible that anyone else could have ever felt this wonderful.

When Bruce's cock slid out of me and he rolled off me, I snuggled up to him like he was Bill. I wanted to tell him that I loved him, but of course I didn't. I knew this was only a job, and getting too emotional would spoil everything. I could, however, tell him that he was the greatest lover I had ever had. When I said this he asked me how old I was. When I said eighteen, he told me that he could believe that was the best I had had, but I had an entire life of lovemaking to look forward to. He was sure that I would have many lovers who would be able to give at least as much pleasure. I asked him if he really thought so and believed him when he said yes.

I started to play with his cock again. He said,

"Don't you ever get tired of sex?" I truthfully replied that I didn't know when I would see him again and I wanted to have great memories of this time. I slid down and took his cock in my mouth. I could taste my juices all over it as I licked the shaft in my mouth. I was pleased I could do this this morning because I couldn't last night, but I was again determined to swallow all of his cock. It seemed to become an obsession with me every time my mouth got near it. I kept sucking and licking, and he stayed soft. The head of his cock was at the back of my throat and sliding past where it had been the night before when he came down my throat. I gave a final push with my face and I could feel his balls against my nose. Success, I finally had conquered this monster. I felt incredibly pleased with myself. Now I began to work on it in earnest. I pumped my head up and down the shaft as I fondled his balls, but he would not get hard, so finally I put a finger up his ass. This had the expected effect and his cock got hard quick, real quick. Once again I couldn't keep it in my mouth when it was hard, but that was all right.

I wanted him in my pussy again. I again straddled him, but this time I pushed down on the entire length in one stroke. He went right past my cervix with no delay at all. Oh, there was a barrier there, but I just pushed hard enough for him to go past it on the first stroke. I now began to fuck him with slow steady strokes. I leaned over and told him I was going to fuck him for a long time so he would be sure to remember me next time he came to the house. He replied that he would remember me until the day he died and I believed him. To this day I am convinced that he remembers that first day with me more than any of the many other times he fucked me. I rode his prick long and hard that morning. I distinctly remember the church bells ringing again as I was still on him. As soon as I heard them, I came as if in response. Rachael later told me that the bells ring an hour and a half apart, so I must have been on him for at least an hour that time.

After we lay on the bed resting for awhile, Bruce got up and said he was sorry but he really had to be going. His wife was going to be back by two o'clock and he should be home when she got there. I held his cock and asked him if he would have any left for her. He said she probably wouldn't care. I don't really understand this, but I suppose it's possible to get too much of a good thing. I kissed his cock and then stood up to kiss him. "Be sure to ask for me again," I said as he continued to dress. When he finished he came over and gave me a long kiss, like a lover would, and told me I could count on it. I waited until he left to go to the bathroom again and make myself presentable.

By now it was almost noon, so I thought it was time I went back to my dorm. When I went downstairs to tell Rachael I was leaving, I purposely avoided going near the "reception" room because I was really totally wiped out from all the sex in the last twenty-four hours. I found Rachael in her study reading again. This time I got a look at the title of the book and was surprised it was Plutarch's *Lives*.

Rachael immediately stood up and came over to me. I was kind of surprised when she kissed me on the cheek as she asked me how I was feeling.

Actually I felt pretty good except for being tired from all the sex. She told me she was very proud of me. I had done everything she could have asked of anyone. Considering that I was so new in the business, she was extremely pleased. As we were talking she led me over to a couch and we both sat down. I felt very comfortable with her, not like I would with an employer in a regular job. After we had talked for a few minutes and she was reassured that I wasn't put off by the amount of sex I had had the night before, she got up and went to her desk. She came back with an envelope (my pay), and a clipboard.

On the clipboard she had broken down how she arrived at the total for my pay for the night. The first three men had only requested regular sex (she didn't consider the mirror kinky), so their cost had been $80 each, which we split. Thus I made $120 from them. I already knew she had charged the group of four that I had taken on all at once an extra $50 each. Thus, they each paid $130 for a total of $520, which we split. So I had another $260 from them. (I was beginning to feel a lot less tired.) Now we came to Bruce. Rachael had told me earlier that she asked Bruce to fuck me so that I would be completely "broken in," so I didn't have any idea if I were going to be paid for servicing him. I had already made $380, which was more than my mother and father combined made in an entire week. I should have had more faith in Rachael. She had charged Bruce $500 for the entire night. She said she always charged that much for a girl to stay overnight on Saturday night. Since I was unavailable for other men on the busiest night of the week, she had to turn away some business, so she felt justified in charging so much. We also split this amount, so my total pay for the night was $630. She handed me an envelope stuffed with cash. I just looked at it for about a minute and then I told her I had never even seen that much money before except in the bank. She smiled at me and said, "Honey, you're going to see many times that much if you keep working here. You are a prize."

I suddenly remembered Maria. I told Rachael that I had promised myself to give Maria a good tip because she had asked the four men to take it easy on me because I was new, and I had really appreciated that. Rachael asked if I wouldn't rather give it to her myself. I thought for a minute and said that it would be better if she gave it to her, because then Maria couldn't turn me down. Rachael agreed to this and I got up to leave after giving her $50 for Maria. (The next time I saw Maria she thanked me for the tip, and treated me extra nice. After this I always tipped her. In the long run it made me money, because she always steered the best customers my way.)

Rachael told me that Jim and Harry (my first two customers) were going to be in town Wednesday night and had called her for some "escorts." (They were aware that I didn't know I was to be paid the first night they met me.) They were glad to hear that I had worked out all right, and said they would be happy to have Cindy and me again, but when Rachael asked if they would like me and a new girl, they said that would be fine. Once again Rachael told them that the new girl, if she came, might now know she was to be paid.

I was pleased at the thought of meeting Jim and

Harry again, but thought that Rachael was pushing Cindy out of the picture. I mentioned this to Rachael (not quite in those words), but she said that Cindy was scheduled to go out with another client that night. This kind of forced my hand. I hadn't even seen Lisa since the night of the party, although I had spoken to her on the phone. The only thing Rachael asked was to let her know as soon as possible if Lisa couldn't make it. I told her I would call Lisa that night.

CHAPTER 14
Back at the Dorm

Even though it was nice outside, I took a cab home because of carrying the money. I was sorry it was Sunday, because I couldn't put the money in the bank until the next day, but there was nothing I could do about it. I hid the money in my room when I got back home, but I was still relieved when I went to the bank Monday morning. It felt great to deposit $500 into my account until it seemed like the cashier looked at me for a long time (probably only about three seconds) when I gave her the deposit slip. I realized right then that she knew how I had made the money. I couldn't see myself, but I knew I was beet red. After that I made it a habit to use other branches of my bank so that I wouldn't have to deal with the same cashier all the time.

To get back to Sunday afternoon, I was greeted by Kathy as soon as I got back to my room. Needless to say she was full of questions. She didn't know that I worked for Rachael. She only knew that I knew someone named Rachael who was a friend of Cindy's. She didn't even suspect that I was earning money by fucking men, and I was not planning to tell her. When I took off my coat and she saw my skirt and blouse, she did say that it was no wonder I stayed all night with whatever boy I was with because I looked so good. I thanked her for the compliment, but then remembered what I was wearing underneath. I wasn't in a mood to explain to her why I worn a corset with stockings and no panties when I left yesterday afternoon, so I went into the bathroom to put on my robe.

She was curious about who I was with, because both Steve and Andy had called. I told her I had broken up with Steve and he could take a hike, but I thought I might call Andy back after I rested for awhile. I was having a hard time deciding what to tell Kathy. She already knew I had been with a man, but I had to pick a story and stay with it. I finally decided to tell her I had met a man named Bob when I was at the library taking notes for history class and he had asked me out. I think she was actually envious because she said, "I go to the library all the time and all I ever meet are jerks. How did you find a nice guy right away? Where does he go to school? Does he have a friend?"

I had to put my hand over her mouth to make her stop talking. By now I had my story worked out a little better, so I told her he didn't go to school, because he was over thirty and I was more concerned about his wife than his friends. Now Kathy was speechless. "Married? That's terrible. Don't you have any morals?" And then all of a sudden, "Tell me all about it. What was his name? Was he good? What did you do together? Where did you go?" I realized that Kathy wasn't so upset as she tried to pretend, so I elaborated on my story to her. I told her we went out to dinner and then he took me back to his hotel room. I even told her that he called his wife when I was there sucking his cock. (Kathy's eyes just about doubled in size with this news.) I was beginning to be proud of my ability to make up this story that she believed totally. "Then, after he got off the phone, he pushed me back on the bed and fucked me for the first of many times that night." "How many times? Was he a good lover? Did he eat you?" "I don't know exactly how many times, and yes, he was a good lover and yes, he did eat me."

"I don't believe how lucky you are. If I got picked up in the library, the guy would have been a jerk and he would have taken his mother along on the date."

I told her that if she continued to think like that, there was no hope for her. "You've got to have better expectations. You are very pretty and lots of men would love to get you in bed. Do you want me to ask Andy to bring a friend for you if he wants to go out with me again?"

"I don't think I want to lose my virginity on a double date with a total stranger. I don't even know Andy, let alone any friend of his. I only spoke to him on the phone."

"You don't have to screw him the first night you meet him, but you've got to get out and meet boys if you want to have a good time while you're in college. You don't have to screw anyone you don't like, but

128

you've got to meet people."

"Okay, sure. I'd be glad to go out with you and Andy. To tell you the truth, I'd really love to meet someone like Bob. I think an older man might be more patient, not in such a hurry to get in my pants."

I agreed with her that was the basic difference among men. They all wanted to get in our pants, but older men were more patient, and therefore succeeded more often. I think she would have been glad to go let Bob fuck her right then, but of course this was impossible because he didn't really exist. I certainly didn't want to tell her what I had really been doing last night, and my sorry about Bob didn't say that I would see him again, so I was off the hook as far as he was concerned. I did decide to start looking for an older man for her, someone who would take it easy on her instead of just jumping on her for her first time. I think Kathy would have freaked out if she had been at our party up on Riverside Drive with Andy and Steve. Thinking about that party reminded me about Lisa. I made up my mind to give her a call that night to see if she was interested in going out this Wednesday.

After Kathy left I took a brief nap and then decided to call Andy and Lisa. I reached Andy right away. He was in his apartment doing some homework for Business Law. Steve was out demonstrating some place. I was beginning to like Andy more all the time. He sounded real happy to hear from me. I kept expecting him to ask me where I had been the night before, but he never did. I appreciated it that he seemed to think my time was my own business. He finally got around to asking me to a movie on Tuesday night. I asked him if he had a friend for Kathy and he said he would see what he could do. (I also told him that I didn't think we would be going to bed that night if Kathy came along, but I would really appreciate his getting her a date.) I was surprised when he didn't seem put off at all by my request, and even more surprised when he called back in less than ten minutes.

When he called back, he asked me if it was all right if we went to see *Promises, Promises* instead of a movie. The friend he had called loved the theatre and would much rather go there than to a movie. Naturally I agreed to this. I didn't get many chances to see plays, and I knew Kathy would like to go. Besides, even if Kathy and Carl, Andy's friend, didn't hit it off, the show would take up a lot of time. We talked for a little while longer and Andy told me he was actually looking forward to just going out with me. He said not to worry about sex for the night. It would give us a chance to get to know each other better. I was starting to like him better and better. Actually, I was a little disappointed that there would be no sex. Even though I had had plenty of sex over the weekend, I knew that when I saw Andy again, I would want to sleep with him. Oh well, there was always next weekend, if I wasn't back to Rachael's. He said they would pick us up a little after seven and we could have a coke and sandwich and then walk to the theater, weather permitting. This was fine with me. It was only thirteen blocks and I like walking around Manhattan. Kathy seemed pleased at the thought of going to see a play, but she wanted to know about her date. Since I knew nothing about him except that he liked the theatre, I told her she would just have to wait.

Then I called Lisa. She was also studying and was glad to take a break. After a few minutes of small talk and catching up on each other's love life (she had been quite active after spending the rest of the night on Riverside Drive), I asked her about going out with two guys Wednesday night. She wanted to know something about them and what we were going to do, so I told her that the only time I had gone out with them, they bought Cindy and me a fine meal at the *Top of the Sixes* and then we all went back to their hotel room. She was kind of quiet for a couple of minutes and then finally asked me what we did when we got back to the hotel. I told her the truth. Cindy and Harry had gone into a bedroom and Jim and I had made love right on the floor of the other room, and I had had my first orgasm; and then we had switched and I had another orgasm with Harry. I was kind of surprised when she said she would have to think about it, but then she giggled and said she was finished thinking and wanted to know what to wear. I told her to dress like she was going on a job interview, not a real short skirt, but not too conservative. Also a little sexy lingerie wouldn't hurt. (Actually she was going on a job interview, but she didn't know it at the time.) She agreed to meet me at five Wednesday afternoon at my dorm. She also said she had no morning classes on Thursday, so we decided she should spend the night at my dorm instead of going back up to Columbia late at night.

CHAPTER 15
A Double Date with Kathy

Andy and his friend Carl met us shortly after 6:30 on Tuesday night. Carl was nice looking, not truly handsome, but very nice looking. I liked Andy's taste in friends. Kathy and Carl seemed to hit it off very well right away. We stopped at a Chock Full of Nuts restaurant and had some burgers and coffee. This was a far cry from the private restaurant Bruce had taken me to on Saturday night, but the four of us had a really good time. I found out that Andy was twenty-two, but just beginning college. Carl was two years older and both of them had served for a year in Vietnam with the army, and another year in Okinawa. I was impressed with this. After all, I had never been out of New York and Pennsylvania. They seemed very worldly to me after this, but neither one wanted to talk about the war itself or what he had done in Vietnam. They only said that they were scared a lot of the time. I guess I was a little surprised when they both admitted to this, but it sure made a lot of sense to me. I would have been scared to death over there.

Andy and Carl had met in the service and become good friends over the years. They had both made up their minds that if they survived the war, they were going to get a good education, and make a decent living. Andy had a definite aptitude for business, while Carl liked the arts. Carl was seriously thinking of teaching at the college level and perhaps writing, while Andy was determined to master merchandising.

They asked what Kathy and I were planning to do with our lives and we told them about Kathy's major in design and mine in merchandising. (Andy seemed both surprised and pleased at this. I wondered how pleased he would be if he knew that my most successful merchandising was selling my own tail. Oh well, there was nothing I could do about that now. I might as well enjoy the night with him and not worry about the future.)

Kathy was looking at Carl like he was a knight in shining armor all the time we were talking. I thought to myself that if Carl wanted, he could probably fuck her in a cab on the way home without much effort. Carl also noticed Kathy watching him. It seemed to make him a little uneasy. Fortunately, it was time to leave if we were going to walk up to the Shubert Theatre. The restaurant we were in was on Seventh Avenue, so it was a straight walk uptown to the theatre district. I was surprised at how dark the avenue seemed at night. During the day the garment center is extremely active and you can't walk down the street without constantly bumping into people. Now it was almost totally deserted. I was glad we were with Andy and Carl, because I felt a lot safer with them, especially after they had told us of being in the service. We did see a couple of rather desperate looking characters, but our trip was totally uneventful because of Andy and Carl being there.

We got to the theatre a few minutes early, so Kathy and I spent a little extra time in the ladies room talking about the men. I was right about Kathy's being totally smitten with Carl. I told her not to fall so hard for the first man she met in New York. There were literally millions of them here.

Besides, although neither Andy or Carl had mentioned other women, I told her I was sure we were not their first dates of the year. (I couldn't bring myself to tell her about the party on Riverside Drive.) I said I wasn't trying to discourage her, and Carl was definitely a nice man, but I didn't want her to expect too much of him and be disappointed if things didn't work out. She nodded her head but I knew she was totally taken by Carl, so I resolved not to say anything more. She was a big girl now and fully capable of making her own decisions. We went out to find Carl and Andy and enjoy the show.

Enjoy the show we did. This was only the second Broadway play I had seen, and I was captivated. I could understand why Carl was so interested in the arts. It must be wonderful to live with this every day. I had seen plays and even musicals performed by our high school drama club at home, but nothing compares to really good professional actors performing on a stage in front of you. Over the years I have seen probably a hundred different shows, but I still like *Promises, Promises* the best of all and not just because it was one of the first I saw. I love the dances and energy of the show. Even when not much is going on and Jerry Orback was just sitting on a bench thinking out loud, you can feel the tension ready to explode, and oh, the dances. I remember one black girl with a green dress and the greatest legs I have ever seen. What I wouldn't do to have legs like that. I wondered that first night if dancers were great lovers. I have since found out that they definitely have great movements, but great lovers are emotionally involved with their partners, not just technically proficient.

After the show Carl and Andy took us to Sardi's and bought us a drink. Kathy and I thought it was great to be in such a famous restaurant with all the drawings of famous actors on the walls. I was sorry when Andy said he and Carl had to take us home because they both had a full load of classes on Wednesday. They got us a cab and rode with us to our dorm. I was a little surprised when Andy paid the driver, because they don't allow boys up to our dorm. He said he knew this, but he and Carl were going to take the subway home. I hadn't realized that money was so tight for them. I guess I had gotten so used to men spending money on me that I forgot most college students didn't have much of it. However, when Andy took me in his arms to kiss me good night, I forgot all about money. My knees actually buckled and I had to lean against the wall so I didn't fall over. As we pulled apart, he whispered in my ear, "I like you a lot. Can I see you again?" I just kind of dumbly nodded my head and kissed him again.

When he pulled away this time, I knew he was leaving for the night. Carl had evidently already kissed Kathy good night, but there seemed to be lingering emotions with them too. Then they turned to leave and I knew that Kathy was feeling as sorry to see them go as I was. We both just leaned back against the elevator walls with silly grins as we rode up to our floor.

After talking to Kathy for a few minutes about what a wonderful time we had both had that night, I almost decided not to go out with Lisa and Jim and Harry the next night, but after I got back to my room a short talk with Cindy changed my mind. I had to agree with her that screwing was the easiest way we knew of to make money, and I would be dumb to do anything that would leave Rachael to believe that she couldn't trust me. When she said it was my duty to introduce Lisa to Jim's talented tongue, I had to agree fully. Every woman in the world should be eaten by that man. I decided to go ahead with the date and introduce Lisa not only to Jim's tongue, but to the world of selling her pussy.

CHAPTER 16
Wednesday Night with Lisa

Wednesday night finally rolled around after a long day of classes. One of my professors (also my student advisor) kept me after class for a few minutes to ask me about school and my plans after school. When I first came here, I would have thought this was just interest and concern on his part, but now I wasn't so sure. Now I've come to believe that almost everything men do is motivated by a desire to fuck a girl. I'm surprised that this doesn't bother me at all. It actually makes me feel more powerful, because I can use it to get more of what I want out of life. I made an appointment to meet him for a conference in his office late Friday afternoon. I didn't want to tell him that I might be working Friday night, because I didn't want to answer my questions about my "job." It was easy to make up a story that would fool Kathy. It might be a lot harder to make up one that would fool Mr. Kenningston. I guess I shouldn't have thought about it so much because if the professors were so lecherous, I'm sure Cindy would have told me. Oh well, I decided that I'd deal with this Friday.

Lisa came up to my room at exactly five o'clock that afternoon. I thought, "Rachael will love her punctuality." She had dressed in a real nice red skirt and jacket with a white blouse. The skirt was tight but not real tight, and the blouse was perfect for showing off her cleavage. I knew both Jim and Harry would be stealing glances at her tits all night long. When she took off her coat, she spun around to show me the outfit. I told her, truthfully, that she looked terrific. She said that I didn't look so bad myself. I was wearing a pale blue skirt slightly shorter than Lisa's with a matching bolero style jacket. My blouse was dark blue because I didn't want my corset to show through. Since Harry and Jim hadn't yet seen it, I had decided to wear it with a new pair of matching stockings. (The first pair were a little the worse for wear.) Once again I hadn't worn the panties that came with the outfit. Lisa said she hoped her lingerie was all right and she unbuttoned her blouse to show me a beautiful red lace bra. She then lifted her skirt high enough to show me matching bikini panties and a very sexy red garter holding up each stocking. I was glad to see that she hadn't worn pantyhose. When I returned the favor and showed her my corset and stockings, she just whistled. When we finally put on our coats to go out she said she hoped the guys would appreciate all the trouble we took for them. I assured her that they certainly would. I was smiling as I said this, because I was thinking that they were going to show their appreciation not only by dinner and some great sex, but with cold, hard cash.

We went outside and I hailed a cab and told the driver to take us to the Hilton. Lisa seemed surprised at this. She said she had assumed we would take the bus, especially since it was only a short ride up Sixth Avenue. I just shrugged off her question and told her it was a lot classier to show up in a cab instead of being jostled around on the bus. She seemed to agree with this easily enough and we talked about what we were going to have for dinner. She was afraid of ordering something too expensive and making our "dates" ill at ease. I told her to forget about it. They had the money and could easily afford a good dinner. I mentioned the steak dinner I had had last time and said I would probably have it again, because it was such an improvement over the school's food. This made total sense to her and she decided to order a good meal too. Our cab was pulling up to the Hilton by this time, so we each took a last look at ourselves in the mirrors in our compacts and went into the hotel. I gave the driver a good tip because he had paid absolutely no attention to us at all on the way. Of course he may have been listening to every word we said, but he didn't act like he did.

Lisa followed me to the bar where we definitely made an impression. We were both carrying our coats and I have to say that we looked as good as any other females in the room. Lisa's red suit immediately grabbed everyone's attention, and my slightly shorter skirt and blue stockings held it. A hostess came over to seat us at a table. When she started to take us to the back, I told her we had to be where we could see the door because we were expecting company. She got a little snippy when she asked me for their names so she could bring them to our table. I didn't know their last names so I couldn't tell her and she seemed to sense this right away. I suppose she sees a lot of girls like me meeting men every day, but I still don't think she had to be snippy about it. Anyway we finally got a table near the door. Since she was so snippy, we refused to order a drink while waiting and only had a glass of water.

I was glad when Jim and Harry showed up in just a few minutes. They both came over and gave me a kiss on the cheek and I introduced them to Lisa. I think it is fair to say they were suitably impressed with her. Jim seemed to almost hold her hand instead of just shaking it. Harry finally got his attention and they asked us if we wanted to stay here or go elsewhere. I didn't mention the hostess' being such a bitch, but said I had bragged up the *Top of the Sixes* to Lisa so we were kind of hoping to go there. Both men smiled and we got up to leave. I noticed the hostess giving us a nasty look as we left to walk over to Fifth Avenue. At first I wanted to shake my butt a little or something to brush her off, but then I thought it would probably make more sense for me to be on her good side instead of making an enemy. I decided to go back another night and apologize. Even thought I had done nothing wrong, I have found that an apology where none is expected works wonders for relations.

Lisa and I had put our coats back on because it was a little nippy outside. As Lisa wiggled into her coat Jim was holding for her, I couldn't help but notice she had a definitely sexy wiggle to her. Plus a marvelous ass. I noticed both Jim and Harry stole glances at her cleavage. I was having good feelings about the outcome of our evening. While we were walking, Harry and I were a few paces behind our friends and he put his arm around me and hugged me close to him. I readily followed his lead and leaned toward him as we walked. I felt very romantic as we walked down the street. Just before we got to the building where the restaurant was, he leaned over and kissed me on the top of my head and whispered that he had missed me a lot. I told him that I had also missed him and had been hoping he would soon be back.

Lisa was impressed with the view from the restaurant at the top of the building. She and I both ordered steak. I know there are probably a lot of great meals on the menu, but I also know I like the steak and I hate to miss the chance for a great meal to replace the school's food. I noticed that we seemed to be pairing off again, but this time I was with Harry and Lisa was with Jim. Maybe it always falls to Jim to break in the new girls with his marvelous tongue. I smiled to myself as I was thinking how Lisa was going to get the treat of her life when we all finally got back to their hotel room. Once during the meal Harry slid his hand up my skirt and put a finger in my pussy. He smiled when he noticed there were no panties to stop him. I was glad we had sat at a corner table where it was kind of dark, because I must have turned bright red when he pulled his finger out and then put it in his mouth, licking my juices off. Jim asked me what was the matter. Harry laughed and I giggled and I said I would tell him later. Lisa obviously didn't know what we were laughing about, but she seemed to be having a good time with Jim anyway. I had a very hard time concentrating on my meal after this. When the waitress came to offer dessert and another drink, I whispered to Harry that I would really rather go back to the room for dessert. He and Jim decided that was a great idea.

We walked back down 54th Street to the Hilton, reversing our trip to the restaurant. This time we walked four abreast and took up most of the sidewalk. Even though it was nice outside for this time of year, we didn't meet anyone on the way, so we just enjoyed our little stroll. I kind of hated getting to the hotel because the bright lights of the lobby always bother me. I always feel as though everyone in the room knows that the only reason I am with an older man is because he is going to take me to bed. Whenever anyone looks at me, I kind of cringe inside.

Jim, Lisa and I went over to the elevator while Harry went to the desk to get a key. I noticed that Lisa didn't seem to feel as much on display as I did, but then of course she didn't know she was hired for the night. She thought she was only there for a good time. Harry got back with the key and we all got into the elevator. I thought we were going to be alone, but just as the door was closing, another couple got in with us. The woman was very pretty and a lot younger than the man was, and I wondered if she was like us. I looked for a wedding band, but didn't see any, so I assumed she was hired too. When I looked up she was looking right at my face. Then she smiled at me and winked. I had to smile back realizing that she was indeed like us. She was out with the man because he was willing to pay her. As much as I had liked my first time with Jim and Harry, I wasn't sure if I would be here tonight if it weren't for being paid. The elevator stopped and the man and woman got off; the four of us stayed for the 23rd floor. I remembered this was the same floor I had been to last time, and Jim led us to number 2312—the same room as before.

Lisa was duly impressed with the room, but was a little uneasy about what to do to "break the ice," so to speak. Jim spoke up and asked if we would like to have room service bring up some wine. Lisa and I thought this was a great idea. There's always a minute of unease when you are alone with a man you are being paid to sleep with, and a little wine definitely helps to break the tension. Harry turned the radio on to a station playing really beautiful slow music. He then took me in his arms and began to dance with me. Jim soon did the same with Lisa. I noticed that Lisa let Jim hold her very close and even ground a little closer when his hand strayed down to her ass and rested there. We were both quite relaxed when the wine arrived, so the glass of wine served more as a stimulant. After drinking one bottle we danced a little more, but much more suggestively now. Harry had his hand on my ass or sometimes on my breast, and I let my left hand wander to the front of his pants. I could feel his cock pressing against me while we were dancing and I wanted to feel the real thing again. I wasn't disappointed. His cock was big and hard and definitely responding to my actions. We decided to go to the bedroom. This left Lisa and Jim in the living room just like Cindy and Harry had left me the first night I met them. I noticed Lisa's hands were also busy. I kind of envied her because I knew how well Jim ate pussy, but I also was looking forward to having Harry's big cock again. The last thing I heard from the living room as we lay on the bed was a "Wow" from Jim as he took Lisa's clothes off. Her red bra and panties evidently had the desired effect.

When Harry removed my suit and blouse, he seemed pleased with my corset and stockings. I know he liked them from the way he smiled at me when he first saw them, and because he left them on as we made love. He lay down on the bed and pulled me down beside him. As we were kissing and feeling each other, I slowly worked my way down to his cock and took him in my mouth. It felt good to be able to take a hard cock completely in my mouth again. I worked Harry over real good and he shortly came in my mouth. I licked his cock until it was completely clean. After we rested a minute, Harry got up and put his finger on his lips, telling me to be quiet. Then he took my hand and we went to the doorway and watched Lisa and Jim. She was lying on the coffee table and Jim was between her legs eating her pussy. Her legs were wrapped tight around his head and her body was rolling back and forth. I knew she was getting ready for orgasm, and watched transfixed as she suddenly screamed and shoved her pussy into his mouth.

Lisa's stockings were still on and she looked really terrific as her legs slowly relaxed their grip on Jim's head and rested on the table. Suddenly she sat up and kissed Jim with incredible passion. I noticed her hand going for his cock and knew exactly how she felt. After I have an orgasm from oral sex, I always feel that I have to have the man responsible in me right then. I just can't wait. She pushed him back on the floor and sat on his cock all in one motion. Harry and I had a beautiful view of her ass riding up and down on Jim's cock. Harry, now still as a board, led me to the bed again. He pushed me backward, so I was gazing up at him as he prepared to mount me. I held out my arms and put them around his back as his cock sank to the balls inside me. I loved the feeling of his big cock moving back and forth in me as he pumped me with a nice slow steady rhythm. After awhile he began to move in a circular motion as well as up and down. This was enough to drive me over the edge to a powerful orgasm. Harry remained hard as a brick and started fucking me again after letting me rest for a few minutes from my orgasm. He was kissing my face and shoulders as he continued to fuck me and I remember thinking, "What a great way to make money."

Then he said something that brought me back to reality in a hurry. He said he wanted to fuck me in the ass. I know I had a scared look on my face because I was scared. I had no idea what to say because I hadn't really thought about being screwed in the ass except in fleeting moments. Harry kept pumping me after he asked me and I just lay there not knowing what to do. Finally I said I didn't know because I had never done it before. Harry seemed surprised at this and I swear his cock got even bigger and harder. He began to kiss me some more and told me it was all right if I couldn't do it, but he would really like it if I did, and he would make it worth my while.

As soon as he said that I made up my mind. I told

him that Rachael would be angry with me if I gave up my virgin ass for less than $500. He looked a little startled at this, but said, "OK, but you're going to earn it. I'm going to fuck you hard and deep." I told him that was the way I liked it in my pussy, so I was sure my ass would love the same thing. He pulled his cock out of my pussy and I was truly sorry to feel it go. He had a nice cock and he was fucking me really well with it. Of course, I was also sorry to have it go because I knew where it was going next. I decided to concentrate on the money I would be making instead of being so afraid.

Harry went over to a night stand and took a jar of Vaseline out of the drawer. It had never occurred to me that he would use Vaseline to ease the way for him. I watched him as he put some on the head of his cock and greased part of the shaft. As I watched this, I was beginning to have second thoughts. I was wishing that someone with a smaller cock would be the first up my ass. Although Harry's cock may not have compared to Bruce's, it definitely was very respectable. I was afraid, and yet I was fascinated as he finished greasing his cock and then took some more Vaseline and put it in and around my ass. I liked the feeling of his finger in me. He moved it around in a circular motion like he had fucked me earlier. I suppose this was to get my ass used to something bigger than his finger. He had large hands but his cock was easily as thick as three of his fingers, and maybe four, so I knew I had my work cut out for me.

He had me roll over on my stomach saying he loved to look at a woman's ass when he was fucking it. After putting his finger back in my ass, he moved it around for a few minutes and stuck two fingers of his other hand up my cunt. I liked this!! I immediately wondered what it felt like to have two men in me at once, but then he withdrew his hands from me and moved between my legs. He moved me so I was standing next to the bed with my head and shoulders on the bed with my ass up in the air. He took a pillow and put it under my stomach to keep my ass at the right angle, and then put his cock at the entrance to my ass. I tensed up, but he leaned over me and whispered it would be better for me if I relaxed. He massaged my back and ass, slowly working the tension out of me, but never taking his cock away from the entrance. When he felt I was relaxed enough, I felt him push. I could feel his hand against my ass as he held his shaft. The pressure was enormous and I thought it would never go in, but finally I felt the head slip inside me. I had to bite my lip to keep from screaming out when it entered me. Thankfully, Harry stopped for a minute and let me get used to the feeling of his cock. It hurt a lot but not as much as I had feared, so I pushed back a little to let him get a little farther inside. Harry reached down and grabbed my tits and told me to brace myself. I knew he was going to ram me all at once. I was scared but there was nothing I could do at this point. I set my feet and shoulders so I could take the force just as he pushed the remaining five inches up me. This time I couldn't help but groan as I felt his balls hit my cunt. Jim and Lisa must have heard me because I heard Jim ask if I were all right. I said I was fine and Harry began to fuck me in earnest. He pumped with long hard strokes and I began to like it as the pain subsided. He was still holding my tits as he suddenly stopped moving and began to fill my ass with his cum. Spurt after spurt after spurt filled my ass before he collapsed on top of me.

I turned my face sideways so I could kiss his cheek as I felt the last of his sperm leave him and enter my ass. He kissed me back and said I was worth every cent of the money. He'd never had a virgin ass before, and it was marvelous to break me in. He apologized for hurting me, but said he just couldn't hold back when he finally got inside, saying it was the tightest place he had ever been. I kind of giggled and said, "You mean my pussy's not tight anymore?" He put one hand under me and slid a finger up my cunt and said, "It's marvelous, but nothing like your ass." After rubbing my pussy a little, he lay down beside me and caressed my breasts and shoulders. I was soon feeling pretty good and started to return his caresses. Suddenly we heard Lisa moaning louder and louder. She kept crying, "Yes, yes, yes" over and over. We just had to get up to see what was going on. My ass hurt a little at first but I was all right after a minute. When we went in the other room Jim was on top of Lisa and pounding into her. Her legs went around his waist and pulled him even closer. He immediately gave a final thrust and froze, pumping his cum inside her. This seemed to be all she needed to send her over the top to her second orgasm of the night. Harry whispered for me to go and join them while he went to wash up, so I knelt down beside them and kissed each of them. I also reached around and felt Jim's balls lying against Lisa's ass. When Jim finally pulled out of her and lay down on the floor, I immediately went between her legs and started licking his cum out of her cunt. Lisa quickly

147

clamped her legs around my head forcing my mouth even farther into her pussy. She shortly gave another heave and had another small orgasm. Her legs relaxed and I was able to come up for air. As soon as I did Jim kissed me and then kissed Lisa again. I couldn't help but notice that his cock was as hard as a brick again, and I was starting to get warm myself. I could hardly wait to have Jim treat my pussy to his expertise, but before anything could develop, Harry came out to join us.

He kissed me warmly and then bent over to kiss Lisa. She responded rather weakly, so Harry said we should have the second bottle of wine to refresh ourselves. We all seemed to need the break from sex, so we spent the next half hour talking and finishing the bottle of wine. I was sorry to see the wine come to an end because I really enjoyed talking with them. I considered them all to be my friends now even though Jim and Harry were actually customers. Both Lisa and I got compliments on our lingerie. Jim hadn't seen my corset before, but he definitely approved, and Harry couldn't take his eyes of Lisa's legs which were beautiful in her black stockings with red garters. He red bra and panties were lying on the floor where they had been tossed earlier. I had to admit that she was beautiful.

Finally, Jim came over to me, took my hand, and pulled me up off the floor. He said he didn't know if Lisa was ready for more action with Harry yet, but he knew I was born ready. Lisa looked sorry to be losing Jim, just like I had the first night I met him and Harry, but she took it like a trooper. She immediately sat close to Harry and began to massage his cock and balls. I knew it wouldn't be long before she had him fully erect. Before I could see this, Jim had me in the bedroom and was gently pushing me back on the bed. He knelt in front of me and put my legs over his shoulders. I thought he would either start eating me or fuck me right away, but he didn't. He just stayed in this position for a minute. I finally asked him if anything was the matter. I thought maybe he didn't like the idea of eating my pussy after Harry had fucked me, but I immediately remembered that he had gone down on Cindy the other night, so I didn't know what was the matter. He told me that he was only admiring my cunt, which he said was beautiful. I hadn't really thought much about my cunt being different than other women's, but I suppose it's possible. After all, cocks certainly vary a lot in appearance, and not only in size. For instance, Harry's cock is beautiful, while Jim's is nice but definitely not beautiful. I decided he had looked long enough and said, "If it's so beautiful, maybe you should kiss it." This seemed to be all he needed to start using his wonderful tongue. Within five minutes of his expert ministrations, my body was racked with a huge orgasm. I remember taking his head in my hands and pulling him even closer to me.

Jim got out from between my legs and lay down on the bed next to me. I could feel his hard cock pressing against my leg and I could taste the juices from my cunt as he kissed my face. Sometimes guys make you feel like you should be paying them instead of the other way around. I thought I had better start earning my money with him so I pushed him onto his back and began to suck his cock. I could taste Lisa on him as I took him to the balls. Suddenly I wanted

149

him to come in my mouth more than anything. The thought of his cum in my throat seemed to inflame me and I still don't know why. I don't know if it was because I was excited by the thought of Lisa's smell and taste or some other reason, but I began to suck him like a vacuum cleaner. He came in less than two minutes, which surprised both of us, but I swallowed every drop.

We both just lay on the bed and caught our breath for the next few minutes. Since it was so quiet in our room, we could easily hear Harry and Lisa in the other room. The first thing I heard Lisa say was, "Christ, you're big." I smiled and wondered what she would say if she ever met Bruce. Jim asked me where I had met Lisa and I told him at a party at my ex-boyfriend's. He wanted to know all about the party, but I really didn't want to tell him that I had screwed four guys the night after I had first met him (actually five if you count Saul at the dress shop), so I said both Lisa and I had dumped our boyfriends after that night because they were jerks. Jim was persistent and asked me if I had fucked my boyfriend that night. I could feel his cock getting hard again so I knew this was turning him on for some reason. Knowing this, I told him that of course I had fucked him, but when I thought for a minute, I added, "That was the last night I screwed anyone and didn't get paid for it." Jim seemed greatly amused by this, although to this day I don't know why.

He was by now fully hard again and moved over me. My pussy had recovered somewhat from Harry's harsh treatment, so I could feel my walls gripping every inch of his cock. Jim is quite athletic and began to pump me with a very steady rhythm. Although I wasn't excited when he began, the natural forces of nature ensured that I would shortly begin to respond to his movements. Shortly I was bucking upwards to meet his every downward thrust. His balls were slapping against my ass with a fury as he increased his tempo. I love the feeling of balls slapping against my ass. Pretty soon he gave a final deep lunge and held perfectly still; then suddenly his prick began to pump gobs of his cum inside me. I could feel every contraction of his prick as it continued to spurt in me. My body was still arched with him deep inside me when I began to shake with my own orgasm, which followed his by only seconds. I grabbed his head with my hands and pulled his lips to mine. I sucked his tongue into my mouth like it was another prick I was privileged to have from Jim. I wanted to feel him everywhere inside of me, but I finally had to let him come up for air. I was actually afraid of sucking the life from him for a minute, but that of course is impossible; it's only how I felt. As his tongue withdrew from my mouth, his cock withdrew from my cunt and he collapsed on the bed beside me. After he caught his breath, the first thing he said was, "Thank god my plane doesn't leave until ten in the morning. I couldn't handle an early flight." Then he rolled over and kissed me, telling me I was a great lover. I kissed him back with true affection and returned his compliment. I really liked this man.

A few minutes after this we heard Lisa have another orgasm from the other room and then silence. Evidently Harry was finally fucked out just as Jim was. I knew it was time for Lisa and me to leave. I kissed Jim again and told him I really loved going to bed with him and hoped to see him again. He guaranteed that I would and gave me an envelope with two hundred dollars. I left fifty there and put the rest in my purse. (Harry had said that he would send Rachael the money for my ass, so I wasn't expecting anything from that. He was as good as his word. The next time I saw Rachael she paid me $250.) The fifty in the envelope was of course for Lisa. I hoped she would not be offended when I gave it to her.

CHAPTER 17
Going Home with Lisa

After getting dressed Lisa and I went down to the lobby and had the doorman get us a cab. Lisa whispered to me, "Do you think he" (meaning the doorman) "knows what we were doing?" I told her I was sure that we weren't the only girls to leave the hotel so late that night and that I was certain the doorman knew, but couldn't care less. But I think Lisa thought that everyone in the lobby and street was staring at her with full knowledge of her actions.

We got a cab right away and headed back to my dorm. Lisa said she didn't have any morning classes so if it was all right with me, she could spend the night. I told her it was all right with me, but I wasn't sure if Cindy would be there or not, so we might have to sleep in the same bed. She said that after all she had done that night, she was sure she could sleep on the floor with no problem. I decided it was time she learned about the money.

"I have something for you," I said, giving her the envelope with the fifty dollars in it.

She looked totally confused when she opened the envelope and saw the money. "What's this?"

"It's a present to you from Jim and Harry. They were very fond of you and the way you treated them. I'm sure they would like to see you again the next time they come to New York."

She still looked totally confused, but suddenly she understood she was being paid for her evening. "Wait, you mean I'm being paid for the sex we had tonight, don't you?"

When she said that, the cabbie looked in the mirror and his eyes opened wide. He was about our age. I wondered for a second if he was a student at one of the colleges in the city, but just then we pulled up in front of my dorm, so I paid him, and Lisa and I went upstairs. Lisa was very quiet on the way up in the elevator, and a couple of times she frowned, but I noticed that she put the envelope in her purse. Just as the elevator was coming to a stop, she said, "We have to talk about this." I nodded my head and we got off the elevator and went to my room. I was relieved to see that Cindy was not back yet, so we could talk in private.

"Did you know we were going to get paid before we went out with these guys?"

"Yes, I met them a couple of weeks ago when Cindy and I went out with them on a double date. I was in the same position that night that you were in tonight. I had a marvelous time and was on the way home before Cindy told me about being paid and gave me an envelope with fifty dollars in it. We came back here and talked about it for awhile. I eventually

153

decided that I liked the two men and if they were willing to take me out to dinner and also to pay for going to bed with me, that was all right with me. Besides, I can really use the money."

"We can all use the money, but I feel a little strange about this. It never occurred to me that I would be a prostitute."

"I prefer the term, call girl. It sounds more dignified."

"No matter what you call it, accepting money for sex is prostitution, and if we do it, we are prostitutes."

"I guess so, but I don't feel cheap or degraded at all. I just had a great dinner and some great sex with two men. The fact that they paid me for my time just doesn't seem that terrible to me."

"I think that's what's bothering me the most. I don't mind the idea of receiving money for having a great time. I guess I just don't think I should enjoy receiving money for sex. My mother would have a fit if she even knew I was out with two married men, let alone accepted money from them."

I told her that both of our mothers would have a fit if they knew about the party at Steve's apartment. We didn't make any money that night, but we still screwed four guys, which was probably more than both of our mothers combined. Lisa was nodding her head as I said this, but suddenly I could see that she had thought of something.

"Have you done this with anyone else besides Jim and Harry? I mean, I know you've had sex with more guys. Have you had sex for money with more than these two?"

I had already decided to be entirely truthful, so I

said, "Yes, since my first night with Jim and Harry, I have had over ten other men for money. I wasn't crazy about all of them, but I did like most of them and some of them could have had me without paying. In fact they still could, but they wouldn't dream of it. They're so used to paying that they would think not paying was too kinky for them."

"Where do you find them? You can't just go up to them on the street and ask, can you? I mean, my god, you might be arrested for that."

I told her we could be arrested for accepting the money anyway, but from my understanding of the law, a cop would always try to get you to accept money before having sex. (I guess they can't legally have sex with a prostitute, so they have to try to get her to accept the money first.) She seemed a little put off by this, so I rushed ahead and mentioned that I worked for a lady named Rachael who ran a very discreet business and only dealt with men who were referred to her by customers she already had. There didn't seem to be a lot of risk to what she was doing and the men were all respectable gentlemen.

"Respectable gentlemen don't cheat on their wives," Lisa admonished.

"All right, so they're not respectable, but at least they're gentlemen, and I like most of them," I said. Then, looking her right in the eye, I added, "and I'm sure you will too."

Lisa was silent for a minute, then she seemed to make up her mind. "How do I meet Rachael, and how does this work? Do I call her? Does she call me? Do the men pick us up to go out or do we meet all of them in hotels like we did tonight? I don't mind telling you I felt a little uneasy going to a hotel tonight to meet a man I had never seen before. I felt really cheap when you didn't know the last names of the men we were supposed to meet. Now that I think of it, that should have been a dead giveaway that we were going to be paid."

I held up my hand to stop her from asking so many questions and did my best to answer them. "I'll take you to meet Rachael. She usually tries to have a schedule set up so that you and she will both know when you are working, but I have had her call me when she was shorthanded and needed help. I don't really know if any of the men ever pick us up to go out. All but Harry and Jim I've had at her house. She owns a beautiful brownstone on the Upper East Side. I really like working there because I feel very safe."

"What do you mean, safe?"

"I just meant that I feel a little uneasy going to a hotel to meet someone I don't know. Cindy took me to meet Jim and Harry the first time I met them. I don't think I would have had the courage to meet them alone. Working in her house is just nice. The house itself is nice, the rooms are nice, and even Maria, the maid, is nice. I really like going there."

"When can I meet Rachael? I've made up my mind that if she likes me and I like her, I can do this. I really had a great time tonight, and I'm not talking about the dinner. I really enjoyed the sex with Jim and Harry. They can fuck me any time they want to. If they're willing to pay, that's just icing on the cake."

I told her I would try to set up an appointment with Rachael tomorrow morning if that was all right with her. Lisa said tomorrow was fine so I went out to the hall to use the phone. (We didn't have phones in our rooms in 1969.)

Rachael was delighted to hear of our successful evening and said she'd be glad to see Lisa at 10:30 the next morning. I told her about Harry fucking me in the ass and she said he had already called her and informed her. (She also said that they had loved Lisa, so if she wanted to work with us, she had the job.) She would be able to pay me for Harry screwing my ass right away, because he was transferring some money to a dummy company she owned. She said she wasn't sure if she could have any customers there that early in the morning, but she would try because she always liked to have a new girl have a man right away before she could have second thoughts. I told her I didn't think Lisa would have second thoughts, but I wouldn't mind a customer either. Rachael said I was too greedy, but she would see what she could do. I went back to tell Lisa the good news.

I hadn't noticed Cindy in the hall when I was on the phone, but I found her in animated conversation with Lisa when I got back. Lisa had evidently told her of our evening with Jim and Harry and that I was setting up a meeting for her with Rachael, because Cindy was telling her what a great woman Rachael was and how much she would enjoy working for her. "Did you know it was I who suggested that Sharon ask you to work with us?"

Lisa answered that she didn't know that at all and was surprised because she didn't think Cindy had hardly noticed her at the party. Cindy replied that she had indeed seen her. "After all, anyone in our business has to be aware of what is going on around her."

Lisa said that she was overwhelmed the night of the party, probably because she had never been with more than one person at a time before, and that was only a few times. "Seeing your date screw a total stranger just minutes after getting back to his apartment was definitely not something I'm used to, but, I went to college to learn and experience new things. I've got to say that I had a wonderful time tonight. I feel almost as guilty about being paid for enjoying myself so much as I do for being paid for sex."

Cindy asked her, "If you feel guilty, why are you going to see Rachael tomorrow?"

"I don't feel that guilty," was Lisa's reply. "Besides I like Sharon and you too, now that I've got to know you; and I need the money."

I gave her a light kiss on the cheek and said, "If you like sex and need money, this is the perfect job for you. You're going to be great." When I glanced at my watch, I noticed that it was after 1:00 a.m., so I suggested we get some rest. "After all, Lisa has to look good tomorrow. Rachael said she would try to have a couple of customers for us after the interview."

"You mean I start work immediately? I have to screw someone right after I get there?"

Cindy replied before I got a chance, "No, Honey, you don't have to screw anyone, but after you talk to Rachael you'll probably want to get started. Besides, there's really no other way that Rachael can tell if you are going to be able to do the job. The day I took Sharon over, she and I shared two guys and she had another by herself. Needless to say, she came home with more money than she left with. You may

158

as well make your day profitable. Besides, it won't be right after you get there. The interview takes some time."

As she said the last sentence, Cindy giggled and looked at me. Lisa had a look of bewilderment on her face, so I told her that when I was interviewed, we all ended up in some three-way girl sex on Rachael's floor. That was what took the time.

Lisa looked a little nervous at this. "I've never really done that. The closest I ever came was the night of the party with Sharon, but all she did was kiss me, and caress me a little. It really just seemed very tender."

I told her not to worry about it too much, because Rachael didn't push anyone to do anything they didn't want to do. I also mentioned that I was beat, and desperately needed some sleep. Lisa thought it was a good idea if she was rested before meeting Rachael in the morning, so we all went to bed. I think we all fell asleep within five minutes of lying down. I had the most wonderful dream of making love to Bill and falling asleep in his arms.

CHAPTER 18
Cindy and I Take Lisa to Meet Rachael

We all got up early the next morning and went to have breakfast at one of the restaurants in the garment center. Lisa didn't have any classes until 2:00 p.m. and Cindy and I were each free until three. Lisa and I wore the same suits we'd worn the night before. I had plenty of lingerie for Lisa to borrow for her interview. She selected a really beautiful light pink lace camisole and panty outfit that would have turned any man's head when he saw her in it. I wore the same basic black stockings, bra, and panties that I wore the first time I met Rachael. I wanted Lisa to be the center of attention this morning.

I treated for the cab to go to Rachael's (after all, I had made $150 last night to Lisa's $50, and that's not even counting the money for Harry fucking my ass). Lisa remarked that she was beginning to like riding in cabs instead of the subway or buses all the time. I told her that it was always nice to ride in a car instead of the train, but it was vitally important that she not waste all the money she made. She looked shocked when I told her I had deposited over $800 since I first met Jim and Harry. Even Cindy looked surprised at this. She hadn't thought I was saving so much of my money, but I really couldn't see any alternative. I wasn't going to do this for the rest of my life, so I had to take advantage of it while I could. I think the fact I was making so much money and only working part-time really convinced Lisa that she had found the opportunity of a lifetime. When the cab pulled up in front of Rachael's house, there was no hesitation on Lisa's part. She wanted to meet her and get to work.

Maria greeted us at the door and took our coats. She told us Rachael was in her study and expecting us, so Cindy and I led Lisa down the hall. I could see that Lisa was impressed with the building as we walked along the hall. We had to pull her along a couple of times because she was admiring the paintings along the way. She had a much better appreciation of art than I did at the time. When we finally got to the study, Rachael stood up to greet us. She seemed genuinely pleased at Lisa's appearance.

"I'm so glad to meet you, Lisa," Rachael said, as she held out her hand.

Lisa took her hand and said she had heard a lot about her and was also glad to finally meet her.

Maria brought in a tray with both tea and coffee. I couldn't help but notice that she was looking at Lisa with very appreciative eyes. Finally she looked at me and just nodded her head as if to say that I had indeed found a perfect girl for them. I wondered if she had looked at me like this when I first came to the house. I was so busy trying to impress Rachael that I'm afraid I didn't pay much attention to Maria that first day. I also wondered if she liked women more than men from the way she looked a Lisa, and decided to ask Cindy when we were alone. I got back to listening to the conversation in the room and picked it up in the middle.

". . . you understand something of our operation here from talking to Sharon and Cindy, is that right?"

"Yes, I think so. From what they have told me, you must run the nicest illegal business in the entire city. I couldn't bear to work on the street like some of the girls I see, but when I went out with Jim and Harry last night, I felt wonderful and had a great time. In fact, I told Sharon that what bothered me about being paid, was not that I thought it was wrong, but that it didn't feel wrong. I still find it hard to believe that it doesn't seem wrong to take money for having sex with two men who I've never met before, but it doesn't. I'm afraid I didn't need much encouragement from Sharon to come here. I just hope everything works out fine."

"Honey, as far as I'm concerned, you can start working any time you want. Let me explain how you will be paid, so you fully understand what you're getting into." Rachael then went on to describe the payment structure, which seemed all right with Lisa. "I want Cindy to meet someone downtown in the toy center in a little while, but you and Sharon can stay if you like and meet a couple of gentlemen who are coming over at 11:30. Now these two men are very straight. The only sex will be sucking and fucking. Later, when we have more time, I will be glad to explain to you the advantages of being kinky. Sharon can probably tell you quite a bit."

Lisa and I both agreed that was fine with us, but I said I was sorry that Cindy couldn't be here with us. Rachael laughed and said that Cindy would be very busy changing the shape of next year's Christmas (1970's, not 1969's). When Lisa and I looked puzzled, Rachael explained that what products are sold to manufacturers was determined as much by sex as by logic. Besides, where kids were involved, there was no logic involved. Everything was basically just a crap shoot. I suppose this is true, but I had always thought of toy makers as being people who loved little children. Now I know that they are just businessmen like anyone else. Actually they have it harder than most businessmen. Determining what toys are going to sell a year from now must be almost impossible. I've since heard that the only group of people that is harder for companies to try to please than children is teenage girls, because the fads go by so fast. I suppose this is true, but it makes me feel kind of dumb. After all, I am a teenage girl. Actually, until recently I never had enough money for companies to be very concerned about what I was going to buy with "disposable" cash.

Cindy seemed pleased to be going downtown. She kissed both Lisa and me on the cheek before leaving and told us to have a great time, and then told Rachael to be sure to check out Lisa's lingerie. (Actually, it was my lingerie but Lisa was wearing it, and I did end up giving it to her as an initiation present.)

Rachael proceeded to do just that. She asked Lisa to let her see how she looked. Lisa promptly took off her jacket and skirt, but I could see she was a little nervous. I didn't know if I should tell Rachael that Lisa had never been with another woman, but I finally said, "Here, let me help you," and then to Rachael, "I don't think Lisa's spent a lot of time undressing in front of other women." I was actually enjoying unbuttoning Lisa's blouse and removing it from her. I saw Rachael's tongue wet her lips in a clear sign of lust as Lisa stood in her camisole and panties with her black stockings held up by the red garters. Fortunately for Lisa, it was now almost 11:30, so Rachael would have to wait for another day to enjoy the pleasures of Lisa's body. Just as Lisa was getting dressed again, Maria came in to tell us that our customers were here. Once again I saw Maria's eyes linger over Lisa's beautiful body. Even I was sorry to see her skirt cover her ass as she finished dressing.

Maria led us into the reception room and

introduced us to Michael and James S. They were brothers who looked enough alike to be twins, but were actually two years apart. Both were almost handsome, about six feet tall and probably 180 pounds with dark hair and brown eyes. Very nice-looking men. For a minute I wondered what they were doing here. It seemed like they could have easily picked up a pretty girl with little trouble, but then I remembered that men don't come to Rachael's because they can't find women outside, but because they want a pretty girl with no strings. Well, Lisa and I sure fit the bill for this. We both looked good and the only string I was interested in was attached to a roll of bills, preferable large ones.

Maria stayed and helped with the small talk for a few minutes before one of the men, Michael, I think, said they couldn't stay too long and he for one would really like to take us to bed. James seconded this and we were led to the bedroom that I first used in the house; the one with the huge double bed. I was kind of relieved for Lisa that we were going to be together, although now that I think about it, she had handled being alone with both Jim and Harry last night just fine.

Lisa seemed impressed with the size of the bed. When Michael asked if this was her first time in this room, Lisa admitted that it was her first time at Rachael's house. This was the first the men had heard of this, but they both seemed pleased. For some reason, James asked Lisa how old she was and she replied that she was eighteen. When he looked at me, I said I was also eighteen. He kind of shook his had and said we would be the first teenagers he had had in over five years. I was surprised to hear this because they both looked so young, but James said he was twenty-nine and Michael was twenty-seven. They really looked much younger. I decided to make the best of what was becoming an awkward situation, so I said they were both obviously living too clean a lifestyle and should get started on becoming decadent with us.

James smiled at me and started unbuttoning my blouse. I noticed that Michael was already starting to unzip Lisa's skirt as my blouse was thrown to the floor. I reached down and started massaging the front of James' trousers as Lisa was pushed backward on the bed. It was only then that they noticed her stockings and garters. Michael was then in a hurry to get her blouse off. He whistled at the pretty pink camisole and panties and then turned his attention to me as my skirt followed my blouse in a pile on the floor. James seemed as pleased as his brother as he pushed me back beside Lisa on the bed. He reached behind me and removed my bra and attacked my tits with his mouth while Michael went to work on Lisa. I was pleased to see that she was not ignoring her partner as he was pleasing her. Her hand had his zipper down and was bringing his cock out. Both brothers had average-sized cocks which we could easily suck to the root. I slithered down the bed a little to take James in my mouth while Michael moved up to straddle Lisa's chest. She leaned forward and took him in her mouth. Knowing that she was fulfilling her obligations to Rachael, I set about to do the same. James was treated to one of my best cock-sucking efforts ever. I held his cock tightly against my tongue while I moved my mouth up and down. It was only a few minutes before I saw his balls tighten, giving me warning of his impending explosion. I was on my hands and knees with him entirely down my throat when he came. I was very pleased with myself when I was able to swallow every drop before any dripped out of my mouth.

Michael was holding Lisa's head and fucking her face like crazy just as I finished swallowing James. Knowing that his brother had just come must have been a catalyst for him, because he came shortly after James began to shrink and slip out of my mouth. Lisa wasn't as successful at swallowing his cream as I was with his brother, but she did a good job. There was no way these men could be disappointed in their morning. At least that's what I thought, until Michael said, "Do you believe this? We've both come and they both still have their panties on." James replied that that was not to be and immediately pulled my panties down my legs. Lisa's followed suit and then her camisole was removed and tossed next to her panties.

Both men were hard again. Michael pulled Lisa toward the edge of the bed and raised her legs above his shoulders. With a single lunge he was in her to the hilt. I felt sorry that she was not getting the same introduction to the business as I had my first day at Rachael's house, but she didn't seem to mind much. James suddenly spread my legs wide and climbed above me. He also sank to the hilt on the first shove and began to pump me with nice even strokes. Even though I regretted the lack of preparation, I was wet when he entered me and I even began to enjoy the feeling generated by his fucking, when he and his brother decided to switch. This was all right with me because I knew we would make more money if they fucked both of us. Lisa didn't seem to mind either, so we settled down to a good long fuck with the both of them changing places many times over the next half hour.

Finally, at about one o'clock they both came in us (I can't remember who was in who), and got dressed to leave. After they left I showed Lisa the bathroom and we got cleaned up to leave. (Lisa had that 2:00 p.m. class.) I told her I was sorry that the men were not as nice as the guys I had had my first time here, but she said she hadn't expected them to be as nice as they were. After all, they were paying us. We had no reason to expect them to be concerned with our satisfaction. That's what we were there to provide them. I told her I knew that, but a lot of the men really seemed to try to give us pleasure. By now we were back to Rachael's office to tell her we were leaving.

After a short recap of the session with the S. brothers, Rachael told Lisa to be sure to call her anytime, because they had liked both of us and expected to see us again. I told her I would be available Saturday afternoon and evening again and Lisa said she could also work those times if that was all right. Rachael was delighted with this and gave us each an envelope. I was pleased to notice that Lisa didn't look inside until we got in a taxi for the trip back to Columbia. (We each made $80. Lisa had a beautiful smile on her face when she added this to the $50 she had made the night before.) I rode with her up to Columbia because I was curious about her feelings. She told me she had had a great time the last two days. The men we were out with the night before and the two guys today were all nicer than the two guys she had been with in high school, and most of the boys at Columbia. (She also liked Andy and had stayed all night after Cindy and I left the party on Riverside Drive.) She said as far as she was concerned, meeting me was the luckiest thing that had happened to her since moving to New York. As she was getting out of the cab, she leaned over and gave me a very tender hug and kiss. I was looking forward to Saturday.

CHAPTER 19
My Meeting with Professor Kenningston

You may remember that I said a couple of chapters ago that my student advisor had wanted to see me on Friday after classes. I was somewhat apprehensive, but convinced myself that I was being paranoid. As things turned out, my first reaction was extremely accurate.

I got to his office about 4:30 to find him waiting for me.

"I thought you might have forgotten our meeting," was the first thing he said to me. I told him I had a late class, which was true, but he should have known that. He ushered me into his small office and shut the door. I was starting to feel uneasy again. I had barely sat down when he came right to the point.

"Sharon, I've heard some very disturbing information about you."

My mind was racing. What could he possibly know? The only person at the school who knew what

I was doing was Cindy and I was sure she hadn't said anything. (When would she find the time?) I didn't say anything because I didn't know what to say. I didn't want to admit to anything that he didn't really know, so I was just going to have to play it by ear and listen to what he had to say. What he said scared the hell out of me.

"Sharon, earlier this week I was having lunch with a man I've known for years. We were sitting near the window of the restaurant. You and another girl happened to walk by and I saw by his face that he knew you. I was a little surprised, because he's a fairly wealthy man who runs a good-sized business in the city. I started to brag about you to him, telling him how bright and hard-working you were. When he said I didn't know the half of it, I had no idea what he was talking about. Sharon" (I wished he would quit using my name and just get on with it), "when he told me where he met you, I was embarrassed and angry."

He stopped here and just waited, so I finally said, "Where did he say he met me?" I was afraid I knew the answer. After all, the only older men I knew in the city I had met through Rachael. I was right.

"He claims to have met you in a rather expensive whorehouse on the Upper East Side. Is this true?"

I opened my mouth, but nothing came out. I was really scared now. I could just see going home to my parents because I had been kicked out of school for prostitution. What was I thinking about? I couldn't go home. My father would kill me. Professor Kenningston was still looking at me. I still couldn't talk.

"Sharon, you haven't answered me yet."

"I know. I don't know what to say."

169

"Sharon, you don't have to tell me if what he said is true. You face is as white as snow. I know everything is true."

I couldn't believe my luck. What are the chances that someone I had met at Rachael's would happen to see me when he was having lunch with Professor Kenningston? Damn, I now had over $1,000 in the bank. (I had deposited all of the money from the day before and $100 from Wednesday night.) I was thinking that at least I could probably get a small apartment in the city and work for Rachael until I got accepted at another school. It didn't occur to me not to continue to go to school. I remembered Cindy's advice very well about preparing myself for life and not assuming I could work at Rachael's forever. Kenningston was talking again so I had to pull myself out of my self-pity and pay attention.

". . . as I was saying, Sharon, I know you are guilty. I am somewhat impressed that you haven't cried. In your position it would be totally understandable, but you haven't. You're thinking about what to do from this point on, aren't you?"

I looked at him and spoke with resignation in my voice. "Yes, I won't be able to go home. My parents would disown me. My father would probably kill me. Besides, it's a small town. I couldn't face all the people I grew up with knowing they all knew I was kicked out of school for prostitution."

"Sharon, I didn't say you would be expelled from school. I said I was embarrassed and ashamed. It's always a little discomforting to find that one of our girls has changed so drastically since coming into our care. I assume that you met the woman who runs this 'house' from someone you know. After all, this type of job is not normally advertised in the paper. Was she a student here?"

I knew this question was coming before he finished talking, so I made up a quick story. There was no way I was going to mention Cindy. "It wasn't a she and it wasn't a student. I happened to meet a man in the library" (I decided to steal a little from the story I told Kathy) "and spent the night with him. He asked me where I had learned so much. I wasn't sure what he was talking about, because I just followed his lead. I guess I'm just naturally talented at sex. Anyway, the next morning after making love again, he told me I should so this for a living. I must have looked at him like he was crazy, because he said, 'No, no, I'm serious.' Then he wrote down a phone number and told me to tell the woman who answered that he had told me to call. I kept the number for a few days, and then finally my curiosity got the better of me and I called the number. The woman seemed very nice on the phone and we set up an appointment for me to meet her. I almost didn't keep it, because I was scared. But, I did keep it. I liked the woman very much and she evidently liked me, because she put me to work right away. I've only been there two other times. I guess one of the three times I was there, your friend met me."

"Sharon, he not only met you, he fucked you with three other men. I'm just amazed that someone who looks as sweet and innocent as you do went into a bedroom with four men at one time and exhausted all of them."

Well, now I had a better idea who my accuser was. It had to be one of the four guys in the gang-bang on Saturday night. To this day, I still have no idea which one it was. I decided I had better keep talking. After all, Kenningston did say that he hadn't mentioned having me expelled. Maybe I could yet salvage this situation. "Professor Kenningston, I know I should be ashamed and apologize to you for what I've done. I am sorry if I have brought any shame on the school, because I really like it here and I wouldn't want to do anything that would be adverse to the school. But I'm not really ashamed for me. I'm not sorry for what I've done because I don't feel guilty or dirty. The only time I've had sex and felt at all dirty about it was with a boy I liked a lot. He started calling me names because I was enjoying myself so much. The men I've met at the house have all treated me very well. I probably would have gone to bed with some of them without being paid. The money just makes it the most profitable way I can think of to quickly accumulate some money. When I get out of school, I want to be debt-free and have some money in the bank. If you'll let me stay in school if I stop working there, I'll do it, but I would prefer another way." (He had stood up and started to walk around the room, and I noticed that the bulge was growing in his trousers.)

"What way is that, Sharon?"

He was now standing right beside me. If his pants had been unzipped, I could have sucked his cock right there. "I thought that since your friend appreciated my abilities, you might do the same." His cock was beginning to strain at the front of his pants. I figured that screwing him was going to be the cheapest way out of this mess. After all, my pussy had gotten me into this situation and my pussy was going to get me out of it if I had anything to say about it.

"Perhaps we could come to some sort of agreement at that, Sharon. I have to leave now, but I could come back to the building later tonight if you cancel your dates for the night and agree to meet me here."

"I have absolutely nothing planned for this evening. Why don't I meet you here about 7:30." He seemed startled that I didn't have anything planned for the evening, but I had purposely left it open when he said he wanted to see me after classes. I had an idea at the time that something was wrong and I might be able to correct it with some "extra-credit" work.

"That will be fine."

I stood up and stretched up a little to kiss him on the cheek. "You won't regret this evening. Just try to be a little early because I don't like to wait around on the street after dark." He nodded his head in affirmation and I turned and left.

After dinner at the dorm (yech), I got dressed to meet Professor Kenningston. I wore my blue corset and stockings without panties, and a short, light blue dress. I thought I looked pretty good and I even managed to get out of the dorm before Kathy or Cindy asked me where I was going for the evening. It was too early to go to school yet, so I killed a little time at Macy's looking at clothes. It was nice to shop knowing that I could really afford to buy anything I wanted instead of just window shopping. I saw a real cute outfit that I decided to come back for the next day.

The time went by fast as I was shopping, so I left to meet my advisor. He was waiting just inside the building when I showed up (at exactly 7:30), and let me in as soon as he saw me. I wondered where he was going to take me to fuck me, but we just went up to his office. Surprisingly, I wasn't nervous at all when we went down the hall and he unlocked the door. I guess I must have felt pretty safe in the building with both the front door and his office door locked. He had barely got inside the door when he turned and kissed me hard, real hard. The thought crossed my mind that this man was starved for sex. I didn't know if he were married or not, but he acted like I was the first woman he had been with in ages.

My attempt to look good for him was mostly wasted because he didn't even turn on the lights. My coat was just tossed aside and my dress followed it within seconds. He did notice my lingerie from the light coming in through the windows. He stopped for a minute and turned me around admiring the view both as my ass came into view and as it was followed by my pussy. I don't think he had ever seen anyone dressed like I was, because he was clearly fascinated. He even mentioned that I was beautiful and he could understand why men would pay for the chance to make love to me.

As he kept talking, I slid to my knees and unbuttoned his pants, taking his cock in my mouth. He was already hard, reinforcing my first thought that it had been a long time since he had had sex. His cock was nothing extraordinary, but it was more than adequate. Actually, he was a nice-looking man. He was at least six feet tall. He was very slightly overweight and had almost no hair on his chest. I couldn't help but notice that his arms looked incredibly strong. I couldn't understand why he wouldn't be getting any sex in this day and age. After all, most girls my age and slightly older don't charge for it. All men have to do is spend a little time and be willing to get a few "no's" and they will eventually bed a lot of girls. I digress. I started to suck on his cock and use my tongue to apply pressure as I pulled him ever deeper in my mouth. By the time I got him completely down my throat, he was ready to come. I was surprised but let my throat relax and was able to swallow every drop.

After he pumped his last few ounces in my mouth, he pulled me to my feet and kissed me again. He began to talk to me telling me how wonderful I was and how beautiful I was. As I said earlier, if a man wants to call me beautiful, I'm certainly not going to tell him differently. He said he hoped I wasn't in a hurry, because he would like to spend a little more time with me. I told him that I fully expected him to come at least once more before I let him get away. (Men love it when you act like you can't bear the thought of them leaving you.) I was fondling his cock and balls all the time we were talking and he got hard very quickly again. I whispered for him to lay down on the floor so I could sit on top of his beautiful cock. Before he did that he started to suck one of my breasts. Once again I began to get wet as my breast was sucked and fondled. When he put his hand down to my cunt and eased a finger inside, he could tell that I was ready for him.

He held my hand as he laid on the floor and pulled me down on top of him. I straddled his waist and lowered myself on his erection as I leaned over to kiss him. It felt as good as it always does when I'm as wet as I was then. He went in to the hilt in one slow movement. I stopped for a minute just to savor the feeling of a prick in me and then began to move as I always do when I'm fucking a man. I was watching his eyes as I began to move my hips in a circular movement. I truly believe that his eyes sparkled when I began this. He held me by my waist and helped me move. He was so strong that I just seemed to float above him as we fucked. I don't think I was on top of him for more than five minutes when he came again. I was kind of surprised because I hadn't expected him to come again so fast. After all, he wasn't young like Steve and Andy anymore. He must have been almost as old as my dad. As he finished coming, I used my pussy muscles to milk the last ounce of cum from his prick. I know he appreciated this because he told me so as we were getting dressed to leave. He asked me how I was able to do that and where I learned it. I told him that it must be natural because they really didn't have a course like that at school, at least not for freshman girls. He seemed to think this was very funny. Maybe he was just being polite, but I don't think so. As we were leaving, he seemed to become a little more worried about what he had done and was very concerned that I not tell anyone. I promised to keep everything quiet, but I had no intention of not telling Cindy. I didn't feel that I had to take an oath very seriously with someone who basically forced me to have sex with him. Besides, I was curious to know if anything like this had ever happened to Cindy. I would have to wait till Sunday night to find out.

CHAPTER 20
Back at the Dorm That Night

After I got back Friday night, I studied and did a report for merchandising. Ha! The author of that book didn't know as much about merchandising as he thought he did. Service was more important than advertising any day.

Lisa called me about ten to ask me about the next day. I asked her if she were nervous and she admitted she was, but when I suggested that she might not to continue working for Rachael, she told me to put such thoughts out of my head. There was no way she was going to quit, she just had butterflies in her stomach like an actress. I told her that in a way we were actresses, especially if we didn't find the man very attractive, and she agreed with that. Then I suddenly remembered the clothes I had seen at Macy's earlier and asked her if she wanted to come down a little early to go shopping. I added that she should probably bring a nightdress and stay overnight tomorrow. After all, we probably wouldn't get done at Rachael's very early and there was no sense in her going all the way back to Columbia alone late at night. She easily agreed with me and said she would see me about ten-thirty in the morning.

After I finished talking with Lisa, I went back to work (school work, that is). I can't believe how much I finished that night. You would have thought that my experience with Mr. Kenningston would have bothered me more than it did, but I seemed able to put it completely out of my mind. I have always been able to concentrate on what I am doing at the time, but when I think back, I find it amazing that I was so little troubled by the incident with him. I knew I would probably have to screw him a few times in the future, but I also knew he would be in trouble as well as I would if the school ever found out about our little agreement.

Kathy came in at about midnight and asked me where I had been earlier. I hadn't even thought to have a story ready for her about my meeting with Mr. Kenningston. She knew about the appointment after class, but she didn't know about our little rendezvous later. I quickly told her I just went shopping for a little while and then came back to study, which was true. It just wasn't the whole truth. She told me that Carl had called and asked her out for Saturday and they wanted to know if I wanted to make it a double date with Andy. I was ready for this as soon as she mentioned Carl's name. I told her that I thought she and Carl should go out alone and have a good time. Actually, I was hoping he would screw her. I think she was too, because she seemed slightly relieved when I said this. She did ask me if I were doing anything tomorrow night and I said Lisa and I had already made plans. I suppose Kathy is a little jealous of Lisa, but if she starts spending more time with boys she won't have time to be jealous. I wondered if Andy would be upset that I didn't want to go along. Oh well, my job with Rachael was really more important to me. If he got tired of waiting for me, I'm sure he would find someone else. In a way it's nice having Bill as a boyfriend, because he's about three hundred miles away. As soon as I thought this I remembered Rachael saying that some of the girls who worked for her were married and I wondered if I would still be working for her if Bill and I ever got married and lived in New York. Wow, talk about planning ahead!

CHAPTER 21
Lisa and I Spend Saturday at Rachael's

Lisa arrived as promised at ten-thirty Saturday morning, looking ravishing, and we went to Macy's. I put the dress I liked on layaway (I didn't have a lot of money with me and I wanted to buy lunch before we went to Rachael's.) Lisa found a real cute sweater and skirt. The sweater really showed off her breasts to great advantage. I also found a scarf that I liked a lot, so I bought that and we left to get some lunch. Since we weren't going back to my dorm, we had to find something to do with our purchases. As we were eating it occurred to me that we could store them overnight in one of those lockers in the subway station at Herald Square. This worked out very nicely and I used the lockers a lot in the future. Sometimes I even put money in them so I wouldn't be carrying large amounts of cash.

While we were eating Lisa mentioned that she had been excited all day Friday just thinking about today. She said her pussy was soaked now in anticipation, and wondered what time we should be at Rachael's. "After all, we don't want to keep all of those men waiting, do we?"

"No, I guess we don't. The first Saturday I worked there, I got there early. In fact I was so eager, I walked all the way just to take up some time. I didn't want to be over an hour early. I remember thinking what an 'eager beaver' I was."

Lisa laughed at the phrase, "eager beaver," and asked if we should be going now. It was past one o'clock so I said sure. We paid our bill, put our purchases in a locker under Herald Square and took a cab to Rachael's. (It was too cold to walk today. Besides, we were both eager to get to work.)

When we got to Rachael's, Maria greeted us at the door and seemed real happy to see us. We could see why when we looked in the reception room. There were four men in there waiting, and Maria said that there were already two girls here, Sally and May, whom I didn't know. (Maria said there was a convention of doctors in town and Rachael was always busy when they were here.) She took us right in and introduced us to the four men there. They were Raymond, Joel, Bernard, and Michael. We must have looked to them like water to a parched man from the way they looked at us. Maria said Bernard and Joel had been here the longest, so she led us and the two of them upstairs to two bedrooms. I was kind of relieved to see that there was nothing kinky about my bedroom. Evidently Bernard just wanted straight sex, which would be best for me since it looked like we were going to be busy today. As Lisa and Joel went into the room across the hall, I noticed his hand on her ass. She turned and gave him a devastating smile. I was sure he was going to be a very happy customer by the time he left.

By now Bernard and I were alone in the room. He turned me around and kissed me. From the strength

180

of the kiss, I was sure that I was right about the men being parched. This man wanted me desperately. As I was kissing him back he was unbuttoning my blouse and rubbing my tits. You know what this does to me. My pussy was getting wet almost immediately. He stopped kissing me for a minute and took my blouse off and tossed it aside. After my skirt had followed it to the floor, he stopped to admire me. I was wearing my original black bra, panties, and stockings. He evidently liked what he saw because he whistled as he had me turn around. I was surprised when he asked me how old I was, but not as surprised as he was when I told him. He said he had a daughter two years older than me. Now it was my turn to be surprised. I didn't think he was a day over thirty-five. I guess I'm a terrible judge of a man's age. I decided I had better get things moving before he began to have second thoughts. I had his pants undone and off in less than a minute. I became the aggressor and pushed him back on the bed, like men so often push me. As he lay there I got between his legs and took his cock in my mouth. I was surprised that he was still soft, because he had seemed so eager when we first came into the room. I had to get his daughter out of his mind.

I had evidently found the solution to a soft prick in his case. He got hard (a nice full eight inches) within a couple of minutes and seemed surprised that I was able to take him to the hilt with no trouble. Every few minutes I would take him out of my mouth and suck his balls for awhile. He had really nice balls. I just loved moving them around in my mouth and smelling his scent as my nose nuzzled him. I was surprised when he started to come while I was sucking his balls. They hadn't pulled up tight against his body as men's balls normally do. I had to move quickly to get my mouth back on his cock so I could swallow the last of his semen. After he finished coming, I crawled up on the bed and laid next to him.

He still had on his jacket and tie, so I began to loosen the tie and unbutton the shirt. I think he thought I expected him to leave, because he had a puzzled look on his face. "You haven't fucked me yet," I told him. "And I always expect my men to fuck me before they leave me." By now his shirt was loose and his tie was off. He had a nice body. It wasn't hard like Andy's or Steve's, but he wasn't overweight. I began to kiss my way from his face slowly down to his cock. I again took him in my mouth, but this time only to get him hard so I could get him in my cunt. As I was sucking him, he pulled me around so that I was straddling him in the 69 position and began to eat me. I always have a hard time concentrating on sucking a man when he is eating me, but it didn't really matter this time. He got hard again just a couple of minutes after eating me. I think he liked to eat women and probably never got the chance. Why a woman would ever say not to being eaten is beyond my understanding, but Cindy and Rachael both told me that a lot of married women think it is dirty and any man who wants to do it is sick. My answer to this is, "Bring on the sickies." When he was fully hard again, I sucked him for just a few more minutes and then turned around to take him in me. After all, there were more men waiting for me, and from what Maria had said, we could be real busy all night.

I took the entire eight inches in one stroke and

leaned forward to kiss him. He began to thrust up to meet my downward thrusts as we fucked each other. I was also rotating my ass so that I could feel his prick all over the inside of my cunt. His movements became more and more frantic and then he suddenly rolled me over so I was on the bottom. I wrapped my legs around him and rode with the force of his fucking. When I began to moan and beg him to move faster, it was just the spur he needed to set him over the edge. His cock was racing in and out of me real fast until he gave a final huge thrust and froze in place. My ass was off the bed and I was kissing him excitedly. I was really proud of my performance. I was sure he thought I had had an orgasm. I had definitely enjoyed myself, but I hadn't had an orgasm. I think I was holding myself back a little. If I was going to continue to screw a lot of men on the weekend, I was going to have to learn to pace myself.

I just lay on the bed getting my strength back as he was getting dressed. As he turned to leave, I ran over to him and gave him a kiss good-bye. I fondled his cock at the same time and told him to be sure to ask for me the next time he was here. He said he certainly would, because he had never expected to be treated as well as I had treated him. "I expected you to rush me out. After all, I know you are going to be busy tonight."

I told him that I was far too fond of men, and especially nice men like him who could really fuck a girl, to rush them. I kissed him again and closed the door as he left. As I was getting my clothes back on, Maria came in and made up the bed. I helped her finish up when I was done dressing and asked her how Lisa was doing. She said she had finished shortly before me, and Joel could barely walk down the hall after screwing her.

"You two girls are going to be a great addition to this place. I hope you never leave. The men always feel totally satisfied when they leave you, and it looks like your friend has the same talents."

"How about Bernard? He seemed to think I was going to ask him to leave when he came in my mouth just a few minutes after getting here. He seemed really surprised when I got him hard again so I could fuck him."

"That's what I mean. You always make sure that a man is totally satisfied when he leaves you. Even with Bruce you totally exhausted him. Most girls are too sore after the first night with him to be more than polite with him. You went right after him again in the morning and screwed his brains out. I'll bet he still hasn't fucked his wife since he saw you."

"That's terrible. His wife will know something is up. She'll know that he's been screwing around on her."

"Honey, when a man has a cock like he does, there's no way a woman is going to keep it for herself. She just has to accept the fact that a lot of women will risk anything to spend an evening with him. So I wouldn't worry too much about his wife not getting enough sex from him. Hell, she was probably glad for the break. I'll send Jack down to you so you don't have to go back to the reception room."

"Who's Jack? I only saw Raymond and Michael with Joel and Bernard."

"Oh, they went with May and Sally. Jack's a guy who came after you left the reception room. Lisa's with another guy named Willis. Both of them have been here before. They're both real nice guys. By the way, your guy's big. I thought you might like that."

"Bernard was pretty big, at least eight inches."

"Jack is bigger than that, not like Bruce, but definitely big. Rachael and I knew you could take him with no problem. We didn't know if Lisa could handle it easily so we made sure you got him. He likes cute young girls, so both you and Lisa were right for him, but as I said, we were sure of you. Lisa will have to come down and meet Bruce some day."

I nodded my head as she said this, and I started thinking of Lisa getting fucked by Bruce. Just thinking of it made my heart begin to beat fast. I wondered if Rachael had any way we could spy on them, like the girls do in *Fanny Hill*. Probably not, but I would really like to see it. I shook my head a little to fluff up my hair and get my thoughts back to earth. I wanted to be fresh for Jack.

Jack came in just as I was getting the picture of Lisa and Bruce out of my mind. I think we were both pleasantly surprised. I know I was because he was good-looking and very muscular. He was shorter than Bernard, but more muscular. Also he was very dark and had a moustache which was jet black, like his hair. His hair was beautiful. It was thick and curly and framed his face like a soap opera star. I was thinking that if this guy was a doctor, his bedside manner must be something to experience. I think I looked better than he thought I would. He probably thought Maria had him go straight to the room so he couldn't reject me first, but I could tell he was pleased with what he saw.

"I'm Jack. Maria said you were pretty, but she lied. You are gorgeous."

"Thank you. I make it a point never to contradict someone who compliments me. Besides, she didn't tell the whole truth about you either."

"Really? What did she say, or perhaps didn't she say?"

"She didn't say you were so handsome."

"Then what did she say?"

I went over to him and kissed him before I answered him. "She said you were big, and that's something I really like in a man."

"Well then, I guess I have a lot to live up to, don't I. Shall we get started?"

He was already taking off my blouse when he said this. My bra was virtually ripped from me, but he was very gentle with my breasts. He sucked them so tenderly that I became hot in less than two minutes. I couldn't stand the suspense any longer and knelt down in front of him to undo his pants. It was time to get his cock out in the open. His bulge was sticking out so far that I had to be careful pulling his pants off. His underwear could barely contain the treasure they hid so I just yanked them down. His cock leaped free and it was truly beautiful. It sprang up and stood straight out from his body. It was a good ten inches long and as thick as my wrist. I don't have huge wrists or anything, but a cock that size is a prize indeed. I put my hands on his ass and pulled him forward toward my waiting mouth. He put his hands on the back of my head and just held it. I worked slowly down the shaft little by little. There was still three inches outside of my mouth when he hit the back of my throat. This was definitely going to take some work if I was going to get all of that in my mouth.

When he said he wanted to use the bed, I was all in favor of it. The rest of our clothes were tossed aside as we made our way over to it. I was kind of disappointed when he said, "Why don't you fuck me first, then you can try again later if you want?" But, the customer is always right, so I straddled him and lowered myself on that magnificent cock. As I started to sit on him, he kept talking to me, telling me to take it easy, he didn't want to hurt me and other things like that. I still remember the look of shock on his face when I suddenly sat down on him in one stroke, taking his entire ten inches. That hurt, because it went just inside my cervix and I wasn't really prepared for it. I just wanted to show him that I could handle anything he had to offer. "Told you I love big cocks," I whispered in his ear as I leaned forward for a minute. He replied that he guessed that I did. We lay quietly for a minute and then he began to thrust upward ever so gently. God, that was a nice gentle fucking for a few minutes. I didn't have to rotate my ass like I normally do because he was so thick that I could feel him filling me everywhere. His stroking was beginning to really get to me. I decided that I had misjudged him earlier when I was in such a rush to get him in me. He was probably just being careful so I didn't hurt myself. After all, Maria had said he was nice.

I was having a hard time keeping up with him as he kept pumping, so I asked him to roll over so he would be on top. I really wanted to wrap my legs around this man and let him go to work on me. I got up from him and looked in amazement at his cock.

It looked even bigger than it had before. This time I got in the middle of the bed and spread my legs as far as possible. He got a pillow and put it under my ass, raising me up so I was a better target. When he leaned over to give my cunt a quick kiss, I suddenly remembered that I hadn't properly washed after fucking Bernard. Well, there was nothing I could do about it now.

I reached down to guide him as he got between my legs. As I put my hand around his cock, I was reminded how big he really was. My hand couldn't reach around him. I moved my hand up a little and rubbed the head. It seemed like the head was half again as big as the shaft and it was really the head that my cunt had to make way for. My cunt lips might close around the shaft, but the head would be sliding back and forth in me, forcing the walls of my cunt to push aside as it gained entry. I guided him to his target and he shortly gained complete entry of me again and began that long delicious pumping that only men with huge cocks can do. It feels like I am being turned inside out each time he pulls back, and then when he pushes forward, it feels like heaven. Jack now began to fuck me in earnest. His strokes came faster and faster. I could feel his huge balls slapping against my ass each time he went in to the hilt. It wasn't long before I could no longer hold anything back. I was bouncing off the bed with the incredible force of his fucking and then I suddenly came. My back arched and I thrust every ounce of my body against him. I just wanted to feel him everywhere, inside me and outside me. I was kissing him like crazy and saying "thank you," over and over.

As I cooled down a little and came back to my

senses, I saw him smiling down at me. I asked him if he were proud of himself. He had probably made me worthless for anyone else the rest of the night. When he replied that he wasn't done yet, I was shocked at first, then it occurred to me that he hadn't come yet. I realized that I still had word to do. "Come on," I said. "Let's see what I can do for you." He began to pump me again with those long slow strokes that got me going the first time. However, this time, I used the muscles in my cunt to massage his cock as he pumped me. I could see that this was having the desired effect. His breath was coming faster and his movements were quickening. I began to talk to him to spur him on. "Come on, come in me. I love it when men come in me. I love the feeling of their cum splashing against my cunt. Come on. Come." Finally, I couldn't feel his balls slapping against me any longer and I realized that they had tightened like they do just prior to a man's coming. My legs were still around him so I dug the heel of my feet into his ass and said, "Come on, give it to me." He thrust one final time and shoved deeply into me, and then he did give it to me. I was flooded with his cum. He just kept coming and coming in me. Finally, I felt him stop and his cock began to shrink. I was now laying on the bed and he was still on top of me and still in me, but his come was running out of me as he continued to shrink. He gave me a very tender kiss and with enormous effort lifted off me and laid down beside me on the bed. We were both totally exhausted. I envied him because he could go get some sleep now, but I had to make myself fresh again and greet some more men. That wouldn't be for a few minutes though. I really needed a few minutes to recuperate. We both just kind of stared at each other. I was the first to speak.

"Did anyone ever tell you that you're a great fuck?"

"Actually, yes, but I know I've never enjoyed a woman more than I did you just now. It's possible I may have enjoyed one as much, but never more."

I replied, "Thank you. Now let me kiss you good-bye," and I leaned over and took his entire soft cock in my mouth. I licked off all the taste of my pussy and told him that now I could say that I swallowed the entire thing.

As he was getting dressed to leave, I sat and watched him. He was really a beautiful man. I was going to have to thank Maria for this treat. Before he left I got up and kissed him good-bye, properly this time— on the lips, and asked him to send Maria down to see me.

Maria came down in a couple of minutes. I was in the bathroom cleaning up a little when she got there. I asked her if I had time to take a quick shower, because I was soaked with sweat from the workout I had just had. She smiled and said, "I told you you were going to enjoy him. Your body may be a little sore and stiff, but your eyes are positively glowing."

"Thanks, Maria, but you still haven't answered me. Do I have time for a shower? Christ, if the next guy's average sized, I won't even feel him. Worse yet, he won't even feel me. I've got to have a little time to get presentable again."

"Take you time, Honey. Lisa's handling two right now, so I guess you can have fifteen minutes to become human again." As she finished speaking, she was standing close to me and suddenly gave me a quick kiss. Then she reached down and put her hand up my cunt, not just a couple of fingers, but her entire hand. "I guess you do need a little time, don't you?" When she took her hand out of me, she put it to her mouth and began to lick it. I also began to lick it and pretty soon we were kissing and exchanging the juices from my cunt. When we broke apart she said, "I really like you and I'd like to have you sometime when we're not so busy." My head was swirling from the activity of tonight, but I nodded my head yes and gave her a quick peck on the cheek.

There was a shower cap in the bathroom, so I covered my hair and took a quick shower. Actually it wasn't so quick. I took a little time to enjoy the water cascading down over my body. When I stepped out I felt almost like a new woman. It's amazing what water does for us. When I looked in the mirror, I was glad I remembered to bring some make-up so I could fix my eyes and cheeks again. I really look a lot better with make-up. Without it, I look like a little kid. With it, at least I look my age. I put all of my clothes back on and checked myself out in the mirror. I looked pretty good. It was time to get back down to the reception room and see if I was needed.

I got there just in time. Two more guys had just arrived and Lisa was still upstairs with the two Maria mentioned. Even Maria didn't know these two men, but they introduced themselves at the door and were on a list Maria had of expected customers. I hadn't thought about this aspect of the business before, but Rachael told me later that she didn't let anyone in if they didn't call ahead first. That way she mostly prevented those types of nights that I had the first

Saturday I was here. The only reason we were over-crowded that night was because two of the girls were sick. No such problem occurred tonight.

Maria brought the two men and introduced them as Nick and Tony. They were both at the convention and looked at me with eager eyes. Just as we were starting to have a little small talk, Sally came down-stairs and Maria made her introductions but had to leave to escort Sally's client out the other door. (Maria always tries to make sure that men going out do not meet men coming in.) As I said earlier, I didn't know Sally. She was a little older than I am, but was very pretty. I thought she was beautiful. The first thought I had when I saw her was, "Thank God, I remembered to bring my make-up." Otherwise I would have looked just plain with her in the room. As it was, she immediately captured the attention of the two men. I like to think it was because she was taller than I am (I'm only 5'3"), but she really is stunning. She's about four inches taller than I am with really gorgeous legs, and a mane of long, thick blond hair. She was very nice to me, but I suppose it's easy to be nice when you look like a goddess. She even had a nice easy way with her that seemed to put the men at ease right away, whereas I always seem to have a little trouble until we get to the sex itself. I was feeling resentful for a few minutes at her ability to totally dominate the room, seemingly without try-ing, and then I realized that if I were smart I would quit feeling sorry for myself and learn from her. I started to watch her movements and listen very care-fully to what she was saying and, more importantly, to how she was saying it. When she finally decided it was time for us to choose mates and go upstairs, I was almost disappointed. Of course, this feeling didn't last long. I really like the men I meet here and I enjoy going to bed with them. Besides, now I was back on more familiar ground. Sally may have dominated the conversation downstairs, but I was going to make Nick real happy he had picked me instead of her.

When we got back to my room, I noticed Maria had the room looking like it did when I first walked in earlier. I was kind of surprised when Nick turned me around and gave me a kiss, which I naturally returned. I was even more surprised when he said he had been waiting to do that since he first saw me.

"I thought you and Tony couldn't take your eyes off Sally, and I can't blame you. She's gorgeous."

"Oh yes, I know that, but you see, I don't like tall blondes. I mean they're all right to look at, but I feel uncomfortable with them in bed. I like short brunettes, like you, especially like you."

I told him I thought that was silly, because he had blond hair himself. It only seemed natural that he would like blonde women.

"Haven't you ever heard about opposites attract?" he replied.

He now began to get more serious in his attentions to me. His hands were unbuttoning my blouse while he kissed my face. I helped him get my skirt off and appreciated the whistle he gave when he stepped back to look at the goods. I decided it was time to reward him with a blow job. I sank to my knees and unzipped his pants. I was a little disappointed at first at the size of his cock, but when I took it into my mouth, I remembered how pleasant it is to such a normal-sized man. It was easy to take him to the hilt even after he got hard. His pubic hair was as blond as the hair on his head and incredibly soft, even softer than Bernard's. I kept my tongue on the side of his prick to increase pressure as I moved my head back and forth. I could feel his hands on top of my head and realized he was unbuckling his pants so he could get them out of the way. I never lost a beat as he stepped out of them and tossed them in a heap at the end of the bed. I'm still kind of proud of myself for that feat. It's not easy to concentrate on a man's prick while he's moving that much. When the pants were gone, he put his hands on the side of my head and I put my hands on his ass to pull him even farther into my mouth. He began to fuck my face with ever-increasing strokes and shortly came down my throat. I swallowed every drop with no trouble at all. When I finally stood up I said, "Well, sweetie, don't you think it's about time we went to bed?" He was still catching his breath, but nodded his head in agreement, so we went over to the bed and fell onto it.

"Did you know this is the first time I've ever been here?"

"I thought it might be because Maria didn't know you."

"Oh, right. Well, I haven't been in a lot of places like this, but this is by far the nicest one I've ever known. It's even better than I was told, and I was told it was great."

Well, we aim to please," I said and then I started to suck him again so he could fuck me pretty soon. I appreciated the compliments about the service, but I knew there would be more men coming before the night was over and I had to keep things moving. I was pleased that he got hard right away and seemed anxious to take me. He climbed between my legs and I guided him into me. I was a little worried because of the stretching from the fucking Jack had given me a little while ago. Thank God I'm so young. I seem to recover quickly, but I was still glad that I took the shower. That seemed to revive me and I'm sure it made a difference. I could easily feel every inch of Nick so I was pretty sure he could feel me too. One other thing I could easily feel was his balls slapping against my ass. His cock may have been normal-sized, but he had a huge set of balls. They excited me by themselves and I was really enjoying the feel of them slapping me as he fucked me. I began to rotate a little under him and thrust upward to meet his downward thrusts. Pretty soon we had a perfect rhythm going and he came in me after a little over five minutes.

As Nick was getting dressed, he started talking to me again. "You are marvelous, do you know that? You are really marvelous. I feel like a million dollars. If you ever want to leave here and become my mistress, just let me know." With that he handed me his business card. He was a doctor, here because of the convention and he lived in the same upstate town that Jim did, only twenty miles from my hometown. I must have done a double-take, because he asked me, "What's the matter? You look like you've seen a ghost." I told him it was nothing, I just knew someone else from the same city, and it just surprised me. He asked me if it was a customer, but I lied and said, "No, only a school friend." I didn't even mention whether my friend was male or female. It didn't occur to me at the time that Jim may have referred

Nick to Rachael's, but after I thought about it a little, that's the most logical way two men from a rather small city would both know this place. He didn't seem to have any more interest in the subject and I was glad when he bent over and kissed me on the cheek just before leaving. I told him I would think about his offer, but to be sure to ask for me again next time he was in the city. (I had no intention of even considering the offer. I liked working here, and I liked the city.) All he said was, "Absolutely," and winked at me as he went out. I hurried to get ready for the next customer. This time I made the bed so Maria wouldn't have to and went back downstairs after freshing up.

I went back downstairs again and was happy to see Lisa. I hadn't seen her since we had each disappeared behind our bedroom doors with our first customers of the evening. I wondered if she had also taken a shower, because she still looked ravishing. She was also happy to see me and introduced me to two new men, Brandon and Willard. I thought the names were a little strange because I had never met anyone named either Brandon or Willard, but that's just my small town upbringing. Brandon was a little taller than Willard, but they were both a little less than six feet. Brandon had light brown hair similar to mine, while Willard's was darker and very thick. Both had light beards which made them look older than they were. Actually they looked kind of dashing with the beards. Lisa said that they had a room at the Plaza and wanted to take us down to spend the night. Everything had already been cleared with Rachael, so they were just waiting for me. To tell you the truth, I was hoping for just two or three

196

more customers and then going home for some well-deserved rest, but I did a good job of acting and pretended like it was the best idea I had ever heard. Besides, I had never been to the Plaza and it would be a treat to go there. I was also thinking of the amount of money I would make because Rachael would consider it an overnight date and charge accordingly. No wonder Lisa was so happy. By the time we got our coats to leave, I no longer had to act to appear happy. I was going to enjoy this.

CHAPTER 22
Lisa and I Go to the Plaze with Brandon and Willard

I love the way Rachael plans things out. It was almost five o'clock when we left her house so she had told the men that if they were going to keep us out all night, they would have to take us to dinner. This didn't seem to bother them much, but they didn't know the city well and asked us to suggest a restaurant. The only restaurant I knew in the area was the *Top of the Sixes,* so I suggested it. It was a good choice because we got a table right away. We even had the same waitress, Nell, that Lisa and I had had when we were here Wednesday night with Jim and Harry. She remembered us and was very nice to us, but that may have been because Jim and Harry are good tippers. Of course, maybe she just liked seeing us out with men closer to our own age. Anyway, we all had a great steak dinner and enjoyed the terrific

197

view. (I'm really in a rut. I've got to learn to order something other than steak.) I watched when we left to see what kind of tip Brandon and Willard left. They weren't as generous as Jim and Harry, so I left another five dollars when no one was watching. I think Nell noticed this because she has always treated me very nice over the years, and by the end of the year she must have known what I was doing with so many different men, most of them significantly older than I was. The Plaza wasn't very far away, but it was cold outside so we hailed a cab and rode over.

Everyone who has ever been in New York City knows where the Plaza is and what a beautiful building it is. I don't care how many new hotels they build in the city, the Plaza will always be my favorite. It has a touch of elegance which is missing from so many of the newer ones. They just seem to say, "Look at the money that was lavished on me when I was built," whereas the Plaza seems to say, "Look at the care that was lavished on me": an altogether different way of facing the world. If the doorman had the slightest idea that Lisa and I were call girls, he certainly didn't give any indication of it. When he opened the cab door, he smiled, took our hands to help us out and called us ladies just as if he had known us for years. I decided I could get real used to this in a hurry. Brandon went over to the desk to get a key while the rest of us waited near the elevator. I'm not sure why it occurred to me right then, but I remember thinking that the reason men always went over to the desk alone was because they didn't want Lisa and me to hear the clerk mention their last names. I suppose this makes a lot of sense, because I know some of the girls in our profession are not above a little blackmail. I didn't let this bother me because it seemed like a logical thing for any man to do. I would have done the same thing in their place.

Brandon came right back with the key and we rode the elevator to the seventh floor. We made a little small talk on the way up and Brandon's hand brushed my ass more than once. I was beginning to think these guys were actually a little shy. I was trying to estimate their ages, but as I said before, I'm not real good at guessing men's ages, and their beards made them appear older than normal. I found out later that they were both in med school and had come to the city with their fathers for the convention. Both of their fathers approved of them spending their evenings sampling the pleasures of the city, so they were making the best of it. I had never thought of myself as one of the pleasures of the city before, but I guess that's a fair definition of the service I provide.

When we got in their room we seemed to have a little lull in the activity. They didn't seem to know how to get things started so I suggested that we order a couple of bottles of wine from room service. They both jumped at this idea and we were shortly drinking a really fine light wine. This seemed to loosen them up a little, because pretty soon we were all talking and laughing like we had known each other for years. From here it was easy to advance to the more important things on our minds. It was almost like we were all on a date, a date that we knew would end up in the bedroom. Brandon was with me and Willard was with Lisa on another couch as we began to kiss and fondle each other like the college kids we were. It's hard to believe I can be paid for doing what I would have normally done on a Saturday night anyway. I was having a really good time letting Brandon slowly work up the courage to unbutton my blouse and play with my tits. I love it when a man plays with my tits. I could tolerate this for hours. He was getting pretty worked up by the time my blouse was totally off and he had unhooked my bra. I noticed that Lisa was in almost the same state of arousal and undress that I was, but she was advancing a little faster on getting her date's clothes off. Willard's tie was tossed with her blouse and his jacket was crumpled under him while I hadn't removed anything of Brandon's yet. It was time I remembered the reason I was here.

I started unbuttoning his shirt and loosening his tie. By the time he had finished with the shirt I was kissing his chest and slowly working my way down. He had almost no chest hair and I suddenly had the idea to lightly bite his chest as I was kissing it and proceeded to nibble at him in a soft, sexy way. I wasn't going to bite him or leave anything as lasting as a hickey, but I could feel the tension in his body when I began to nibble on the skin on his stomach. I whispered to him not to worry: "I won't leave any marks for anyone else to see. I'm just going to make you feel great." He relaxed after this and I worked my way down to the waistband of his pants. I glanced at Lisa and Willard. His hands were up her skirt and hers were inside his pants. Just looking at them got me hotter. It was time that we all went to the bedroom.

The bedroom had two big beds. Lisa and Willard fell on the first one while Brandon and I went to the far one. Both Lisa's and my skirts were tossed aside and we were left in only our lingerie. I was surprised to learn that we had dressed almost the same under our skirts and blouses. We both had on front hook bras, bikini panties and stockings. The only real difference was hers were a pale blue and mine were black. I thought we both looked great. Evidently the men did too, because they both whistled at us when we tossed the skirts aside. I took off my bra and panties and climbed onto the bed with Brandon. I decided it was time he lost those pants and got down to business. Lisa left her panties on but attacked Willard's belt with the same determination I was showing Brandon. I left Brandon's underwear on for a few minutes as I rubbed his cock and balls through them. I also used this time to let him play with my tits some more. Just the short walk to the bedroom had cooled me down a little, so I was glad to have him suck my tits to get me hot again. He kept saying I had beautiful breasts and worked them over real well. I figured his girlfriend was either flat-chested or a prude. Well, I was neither and I was definitely enjoying his attention. If his girlfried was a prude, she was missing some great treatment as far as I was concerned. This guy really loved my tits. After about ten minutes of pure enjoyment on my part, I thought I had better get down to business. I moved down to take off the last of his clothes.

Lisa already had Willard's cock in her mouth when I began sucking Brandon's hard prick. His cock was only average in size, but I went after it like it was the best thing I had ever seen or dreamed about. Neither Brandon nor Willard made any effort to turn us so they could eat us while we were sucking them, but that was all right with me. I was really enjoying sucking Brandon's cock and I know he was enjoying the attention it was receiving. As I felt Brandon get closer and closer to his orgasm, I heard Willard begin moaning and saying, "Oh my God, oh my God." Lisa was draining the last drops of cum out of his cock and the sound of his friend coming caused Brandon to follow suit. My mouth was suddenly filled with his first eruption of the night. I forced my mouth to the very base of his cock and easily swallowed every drop he pumped into me.

It was funny. We had done all the work, but it was the guys who were breathing hard. Lisa and I both moved up to lie next to them. I was kissing my man when I heard Lisa exclaim, "Look, Sharon, they're both hard. Should we switch now or do you want to finish making love to each one first?"

"I want my lover inside me first, and then I want to sample yours as well," I replied. By calling Brandon my lover, I was adding to the illusion that we were just two couples having a great time, not two guys and two girls in a business arrangement. Everybody seemed to accept the phrase so I thought the illusion must be working with them as well as me. Of course, it's possible that they weren't paying any attention to what I was saying at the time. I guess it was probably me that liked the idea of spending the time with two lovers instead of two customers.

Being young, both Brandon and Willard quickly regained their erections and I decided to put my words into action. I climbed on top of Brandon and eased his cock into me. My pussy was still soaked from the excitement of sucking him and his sucking my breasts. I leaned forward, dangling my tits in his face while I rode his cock. He got the message right away and once again paid them the attention they so craved. Lisa followed my lead, so anyone walking in would have seen each bed occupied by a girl straddling a man and making love to him. I was really getting into the spirit of this and rotating my ass to increase the friction of Brandon's prick in my cunt when Lisa said, "Switch," and hopped off Willard and climbed onto my bed. I quickly followed suit and left Brandon to join Willard. By the time I was lowering myself onto his cock, Lisa was already moaning in pleasure from Brandon.

Willard had a lot of hair on his chest and his pubic hair was much heavier than Brandon's, so fucking him felt a lot different than fucking Brandon. When I leaned forward, my tits would brush his hair ever so lightly and send shivers through me. My nipples were still sanding straight out in passion from the sucking Brandon had given them but Willard didn't suck them. He just took one in each hand and began to rub the nipples between his thumb and fingers. This was just the right amount of pressure to send me over the edge. I quickly had an orgasm and froze above Willard. When I recovered a little, everyone was real quiet and just staring at me. Finally Lisa began to move a little faster and said, "Pay not attention to Sharon. She does that all the time." We all had a good laugh.

I guess the two guys must have gotten tired of being passive about now because Lisa and I were both rolled over on our backs at about the same time. Willard slipped out of me for a minute, but that was understandable because I was completely soaked and very slippery. I guided him right back in and he began to fuck me like a man who knew what he wanted from a woman, and was about to get it. I didn't have to look to know that Brandon was also pounding the hell out of Lisa, because I could hear their bodies slapping together just as mine was with Willard. I was bouncing off the bed with each stroke and I was sure Lisa was doing the same. I decided to concentrate on giving my man his pleasure and ignore everything else for awhile. I wrapped my legs tightly around his waist and dug my heels into his ass. I also began to use the muscles in my cunt to massage his prick as well as I could considering the speed at which it was racing in and out of me. I was shortly rewarded with the treasure I wanted as he slammed into me real hard and then just held perfectly still, still that is except for the pumping of his cock in my cunt. I felt his juices spray against my walls with incredible force, and then his cock was spent and it shrunk back to normal size as we lay panting back on the bed.

After this episode we were all a little drained, so we got dressed and called room service for more wine and some sandwiches. To tell you the truth I was so hungry I could have eaten another entire meal, but I decided it wouldn't be very ladylike to stuff myself twice in one night with our "dates." (Ladylike!!! After what we just did, what was I thinking of?)

Lisa and I went to the bathroom when the sandwiches arrived. Neither one of us felt like having a busboy leering at us, so we used the time to freshen up a little. After he left we all attacked the sandwiches, which were very good. I was starting to feel pretty good by the time we finished. It just seemed natural when Brandon and Willard began to converse and ask us about ourselves. They were surprised that we were both in college and only doing this part-time. Brandon said his girlfriend was three years older than me and she didn't know anything compared to the two of us. I told him it was only fair to say that Lisa and I had really learned a lot in the last few weeks. (Although Lisa had only started to work for Rachael, she had been to a couple of more parties at Columbia and picked up some experience there.) He said that that wasn't it. Judy, his girlfriend, just didn't seem to enjoy sex the way we did. In fact we were the first two girls he had ever met who enjoyed sex as much as a man, and he was surprised because he didn't think we would be anything like we were.

Lisa asked what he meant by that. It was just curiosity on her part. Willard said he agreed with Brandon. When their fathers had told them they had arranged for them to spend time in the best "house" in the city, neither of the boys were impressed or much in favor of going. But their fathers had insisted and so they ended up at Rachael's, but had decided to bring two girls back to this room instead of staying at the house. Willard said the reason their fathers were so insistent they go to the house, was because they were both getting rather serious with their girlfriends and Willard thought that his father wanted him to wait a while before getting married. Brandon didn't say anything while Willard was talking, but he did nod his head a few times, so I knew his story was about the same.

I was personally glad that they had come to Rachael's and told them so. "In fact I hope you come a lot in the future, even if you do get married right away."

Brandon surprised me with the speed of his response. "Well, this worked as far as I'm concerned. I didn't know there were girls like this around either. I've been so busy studying to be a doctor that I haven't paid much attention to the women at college. When Judy started to pay a lot of attention to me, I just went along with it out of convenience. We kind of stayed together because I wasn't looking for anyone else. I did go into Boston a couple of times and pick up a hooker and I hated it. I was afraid you girls were going to be like they were, but you are barely the same species, let alone like them."

I had to laugh at the phrase "same species." I loved that. I immediately thought of how much Rachael would appreciate it when I told her. "Thanks. I like to be appreciated for my work," I told him.

"Believe me, you are." This was Willard talking now. "Do you mind if I ask you how you got started in this? You said you've both only been at it for a few weeks."

Lisa answered this before I had a chance. I guess she probably needed to talk to someone about what she was doing and it might as well be a customer. "Sharon invited me out on a double date last Wednesday night. We had a marvelous dinner and a great time back in the men's hotel room. At the time I had no idea I was going to be paid. I did know that the men were married, but that didn't both me much. After all, I wasn't looking for a serious relationship with anyone. I'm only a freshman and I was only interested in having a good time for the night. The thought of a free meal, a good free meal, definitely appealed to me too, but I would have gone just for the experience. When we were in the cab going home, Sharon handed me an envelope with money in it. I was totally shocked. It had never occurred to me that I would be paid for having such a great time. Like you, I had always equated sex for money with the girls who work the streets. I had never really thought about how different call girls were. The next day I went up to meet Rachael, and the rest is history."

"Do you really like what you are doing?" Willard asked her. "I mean, do you really like going to bed with someone you just met, someone you don't even know?"

"Did I act like I was distressed by my work while we were in the bedroom? I think I can speak for Sharon when I say that we love the work. Besides, not only do we get paid for sex with nice men, but we get paid very well. Let's face it. If I weren't here with you two guys, I would probably be spending Saturday night alone or with some jerk, or maybe even a nice guy, from school. I'd end up in a cheap university room being pressured to have sex and have to pretend that I enjoyed it. With you I didn't have to pretend. I did enjoy it. I think it's partially because the tension is gone because we all know what's going to happen. When you hired us, you knew we would go to bed with you, and when we left with you, we knew we would be spending a lot of time in bed. We don't have to worry about you not calling us next day, because you can't. You can only call Rachael. You can ask for us, but there's no rejection for us if you don't call. I just assume you're not in the city or you have other things to do. I sincerely hope you do ask for us again, but if you don't, I won't spend days at the telephone waiting for your call. As far as I'm concerned, this is a great job. I love it."

Both Brandon and Willard looked at me as if to ask if I felt the same way. "I've got to admit that everything Lisa said makes a lot of sense. I hadn't examined my reasons for enjoying the job so much, but I think she's right. But I think the money is more important to me than it is to Lisa, because her family is better off than mine."

Willard immediately looked directly at me when I said this and asked, "Your family. What would they say if they ever found out about this?"

I must have wanted to tell someone about my meeting with Mr. Kenningston because I immediately told them about him finding out about me working in a "house" and how scared I was that I was going to be expelled from school. I even told them how I had temporarily solved the problem by screwing him on his office floor. Lisa was shocked when she heard this, and wondered why I hadn't mentioned it earlier in the day. I told her I had just shut it out of my mind and really hadn't thought about it today until right now. Brandon asked if I hadn't told Rachael yet. I said that I hadn't even seen Rachael today, let alone talked to her. Besides, I didn't see what she could do to help me.

"Think about it for a minute," he said. "What that guy did is as illegal as what you are doing, so you've really got him in as bad of a position as he has you. The guy who mentioned seeing you here is never going to testify for him, so it would just be his word against yours. Plus, I'll bet that the woman you work

208

for knows some people who can help you."

"What do you mean, help me? You don't mean having someone hurt Mr. Kenningston, like in a gangster movie, do you? I'm mad at him, but I wouldn't want him hurt or anything."

"No, no. What I meant was I'll bet that Rachael knows someone who can tape record an entire episode if you screw him again. That way you will have proof of what he did and as soon as he knows that, he won't threaten you again. Just let him know that you will send a copy of the recording to his wife."

"I'm not sure he's married."

"OK, then say you'll send a copy to the school administration. They'll recognize his voice long before they recognize yours. If that doesn't scare him, send a copy to a reporter at one of the papers. That would ruin his reputation and the school would have to fire him."

I thought this over for a few minutes and then told Brandon that he was pretty smart.

"Nah, if I were really smart, I'd have you back in the bedroom, fucking your brains out, not sitting around talking the night away."

Lisa was already standing up and pulling Willard off the couch. "Personally, I think that's a great idea. Actually, both are great ideas. Recording that professor getting his jollies and going back in the bedroom."

Lisa was positively voracious as she pushed Willard back on the bed and attacked his belt and zipper. Brandon and I kind of fell on the bed together. He removed my clothes almost immediately and began to kiss my body all over. I was getting seriously hot as he licked my breasts all around, slowly working his way to the nipples. By the time he finally began to give them some attention, they were sticking out like buttons to be pushed and incredibly sensitive. As soon as he touched them, I jumped and then grabbed his head, pulling him tight to my chest. He responded by sucking on them like a starving baby. All of a sudden I felt an orgasm coming on and clung to Brandon even harder than before. I couldn't believe I was having an orgasm from just having my breasts sucked, but I was. As soon as it subsided enough for me to make out what was going on in the room, I saw Brandon looking down at me with total fascination. I just grabbed him and rolled him over on the bed, straddling his cock in the same motion. I didn't say anything at all. I just lowered myself over his erection and took him in one stroke. When I began to pump him, he definitely got the message and started slamming into me. The force of his fucking was bouncing me up and down above him. I actually began to wonder if he was going to be black and blue from the force of this incredible bout of fucking. When that thought crossed my mind I wondered what his girlfriend would say about bruises on his legs and hips. The thought made me smile. She should try it sometime.

Brandon saw the smile and asked me what was so funny. I had a hard time telling him what I was thinking about because I could only say about two words between his thrusts ("I was... thinking what... your... girlfriend would... say about... bruised legs and hips."), but I finally made him understand what had amused me. He smiled at this and said right now he didn't care what she thought. He may have said he didn't care, but just mentioning her seemed to make him pound into me even harder. It was only a couple of minutes later that he came.

After he had pumped his last ounce of cum into my cunt, we laid back on the bed and watched Lisa and Willard. Next to fucking a man I like watching a man and woman fuck. It's just the most incredible thing being in the same room as another couple when they are fucking so hard that they are oblivious to everything else in the world. Lisa was again on her back with her legs over her man's shoulders. Willard was resting his weight on his knees and hands so that he had a lot of force when he hammered into her pussy. Both Lisa and I still had our stockings on and she really looked beautiful with her legs up around his neck like they were, as the rest of her was naked under his beautiful body. Suddenly I said, "Let's join them." Brandon looked at me a little funny but got up with me and went over to the other bed.

We helped them get turned a little on the bed so that they were lying across it instead of lengthwise. Now Lisa's head was hanging over the edge of the bed while Willard continued fucking her. Brandon took advantage of this and eased his cock into her mouth. I was really impressed that Lisa could suck cock so well while being fucked so hard. She took Brandon to the hilt with absolutely no problem and began licking him like he was the last morsel in a starving world. I decided to give Willard something to think about besides the obvious delights of Lisa's cunt.

I got on the bed behind them and began licking Willard's balls as he pumped into Lisa. A couple of times he pulled back so far that his prick came completely out of her. I used these opportunities to lick his cock and then guided him back into her. There is something inherently beautiful about being close up and watching a good friend being fucked by a man she obviously likes. I was beginning to think that these two were never going to come when I had an idea. It had been some time since I had put my finger up a man's ass to make him come quicker. I now wondered if it would work with both of them, so I maneuvered so I could comfortably attack both of their asses at the same time. Since both were sweating profusely, I found it easy to install a finger in each of their asses. I heard Lisa moan, "Yes, oh yes," so I continued to push farther and farther into her and Willard. It wasn't long before her legs tightened around his neck and she had a thunderous orgasm. As it was subsiding I pulled my fingers out of both of them and again began sucking Willard's balls. This time it had the desired effect and the combination of my finger leaving his ass, Lisa's cunt walls contracting on his cock, her legs squeezing him and my tongue on his balls sent him over the edge. (If it hadn't I would have wondered if he were really alive.) He had an explosive orgasm and rammed so hard into her that Brandon had to hold her shoulders on the bed. Poor Brandon, I thought, wondering what had happened to Lisa's cocksucking ability when she was having that orgasm. I looked at him to see how he was doing and he seemed very pleased so I thought he must be all right. I kind of whispered the words, "Come here," to him and he came over to where I was. I took his cock into my mouth and started sucking him hard. When he was real hard again and grabbed my head to hold it while he fucked my mouth, I put a finger up his ass just as I had Willard and Lisa. This sent him over the edge and he filled my mouth with his cum. It was easy to swallow because this was the fourth time he had come that night.

This episode of fucking and sucking had taken a lot longer than I thought. When I looked at my watch, I noticed it was after one in the morning. Lisa and I had been fucking for almost twelve hours straight now, except for our breaks for dinner and sandwiches with these two men. My cunt should have been sore, but i wasn't. I was just dead tired. We were evidently all dead tired because we all just piled on the one bed and kind of cuddled together. We were asleep within five minutes.

I awoke in the morning to find Willard rubbing my breasts in an incredibly erotic manner. The touch was so light that I didn't wake up when he first started. I was having a delicious dream about lying on a beach while Bill fondled my breasts. When I did wake up I wondered if I had mentioned Bill's name. I hoped not because it would be embarrassing to mention his name while I was with another man, or in this case, men. I guess I hadn't because Willard didn't say anything. He just smiled at me and asked if I wanted to take a shower with him. I thought this was a great idea and we got up and headed for the bathroom.

I was remembering the shower I took with Bill and Jack just a few short weeks ago. I couldn't believe all that I had done in those few weeks and I had a smile on my face that Willard noticed. When he asked me what I was thinking about, I told him I was just remembering how much I loved showering with young men and I especially liked where it led. He said, "Where is that?" So I showed him. I soaped every part of his body and then put a towel on the floor, knelt and took him in my mouth. I was sucking away on his cock as the water cascaded over us when the shower curtain opened. It only startled me for a second and I didn't miss a beat. Lisa and Brandon politely asked if they could join us. I glanced up at Willard. He had his eyes closed and was only nodding his head in answer. That was good enough for them. They climbed into the shower with us and I was pulled to my feet. "We've got plenty of time for that, Honey," Brandon said. I was shocked that he called me "Honey," but I liked it.

He had taken the soap and was slowly washing Lisa's beautiful back. I had never noticed her back before, but she is gorgeous everywhere. I had never even thought of a back as erotic, but Lisa's was so classically beautiful that I made up my mind to spend some time giving her a very sensual massage when we had some time to ourselves (Ha, ha). Willard had recovered from my abrupt leaving of sucking his cock and was now washing Lisa's front as carefully as he had done mine earlier. I took another cloth and soaped up Brandon's ass and legs, just teasing his cock and balls as I washed between his legs. By the time he handed the soap to Lisa for her to wash his front, his cock was pointing directly at her. I could actually see her breathing get deeper and deeper as she first looked at his cock and then started to wash it. I noticed that she still had one hand holding Willard's cock too, so it was no wonder she was getting so hot. I know I got real hot taking a shower with both Bill and Jack, so I new just how she felt.

By now everyone was as clean as we were every going to get so I suggested that we all go back to the bed and have at least one more session there. Everyone seemed pleased with that idea so we got out to dry off. Actually drying off took quite a few minutes because we used the time to playfully arouse each other. It was hard to believe that these men were actually customers for us, and originally reluctant customers at that. I actually felt like I was out on a date with a friend and a couple of nice guys. Everything just seemed so natural with them that I was enjoying every minutes of the night and day.

They had to leave by eleven to catch a plane for upstate with their fathers so we kind of had to rush when we finally got to the bed. We all piled on one of the beds and began by spreading ourselves out in a circle. I had never done anything like this before. I mean I had had sex with two men and even with another woman on the bed, but never with all four bodies linked together. Lisa's mouth was on Brandon's hard cock while his mouth was eating my pussy. He was really pretty good, not as good as Bill or Jim, but earlier I thought neither of them had ever eaten a girl before because they both had avoided eating either Lisa or me all last night. It was really nice to have one man eating you as you sucked another's cock. The feeling of his beard on my cunt was having serious consequences. I wondered if Lisa enjoyed it as much a I did, because while I was sucking Willard's cock, he was eating Lisa's pussy, so we had this perfect circle of oral sex all around the bed.

I was definitely going to try this again and again and again.

All of a sudden Lisa said, "I'll race you to see who can make her man come first."

"No fair. You know I can't concentrate while I'm being eaten," I replied.

"Tough," was all she said. Her actions spoke much louder than any words she could have used. Actually her mouth was too full to speak hardly anything. She was setting about her dare with full expectation of winning. I decided that I had better get busy if I didn't want to be totally embarrassed. I began to suck on Willard's cock like my life depended on it. As my nose descended into his pubic hair over and over the smell of his sex turned me on more and more. I decided to see if I could take his balls as well as his cock into my mouth. I held my hand under them as I continued to suck him, thus holding them up as far as possible. When my mouth was down as far as possible, I licked them and tried to use my tongue to bring them into my mouth, but I was a dismal failure. There just didn't seem to be any way I could get them in my mouth with his cock. Just as I was beginning to lose heart, Lisa shouted, "I win," and pulled off Brandon's cock for a minute, allowing me to see the cum spurt high into the air before she again swallowed it and all the rest that he pumped out. While he was coming so hard, Brandon had stopped eating my pussy and I tried harder to make Willard come. Evidently hearing Brandon's release spurred him on to his climax, because he erupted in my mouth so hard I could not swallow it all quick enough. Some dribbled out, proving that he had indeed come. However, Lisa did win her contest.

I congratulated Lisa on being a great cocksucker. This seemed to please the guys immensely because they both laughed heartily. "I've never heard cocksucker used as a compliment before," said Willard, "but as long as we are complimenting here, I have to say that you have both sucked both of us and I thought you were both great. Far and away the best I've ever had."

"I have to agree with everything Willard said," said Brandon. "You two girls are great in every department. I enjoyed the straight sex more with you than I do with Judy, but the way you so eagerly suck cock is out of this world. She wouldn't even dream of going down on me, let alone enjoying it."

I was thinking to myself that if these two guys took a little initiative and went down on their girlfriends, the girls would probably be willing to at least try, but since they hadn't gone down on us until this morning after we all got out of the shower I wasn't sure if I should bring it up. I decided to go ahead with it. "I'm not so sure about that. I'll bet that if you were all in a nice hotel room like this one, all kinds of nifty things could happen. Don't be afraid to start things. There doesn't seem to be any reluctance by the girls at either my school or Lisa's to suck men, but I do like it when they go down on me too."

"I suppose it's worth a shot," said Brandon. "I think the hotel room might make a difference. The whole mood is different when you're in a place like this. To tell you the truth, I wish I had met you somewhere else, so we could have a normal relationship." He must have caught the quick look I shot at him because he immediately followed up by saying, "I didn't mean any offense. It's just that if I should ever see you anywhere else, my first thought would be meeting you at Rachael's and bringing you here. I'm afraid I could never have just a friendly relationship with you. Sex would always be predominant in my mind when I'm around you."

I think I shocked him to his very toes when I said, "That's all right. Sex is always predominant in my mind when I'm with a man. I don't even try to imagine being friends with a man. Lisa is my friend. Kathy is my friend. Cindy is my friend. But men, they're not my friends, they're my lovers. I like things just the way they are. I'm sure if I ever see you again, the first thing I will think about will be the marvelous four-way sex we just had. Believe it or not, this is the first time I've ever been in a circle like this. It was a lot of fun. Then I'll think of the wonderful evening in the bedroom last night. Then if I think hard enough, I may remember the dinner we had. But first of all, I'll remember the sex. I guess what you're really trying to say is that you can't think of us like you think of Judy and . . ." I looked at Willard because I didn't remember him mentioning his girlfriend's name. He said, "Alice." I continued on, ". . . right. Alice, because we're call girls and nice girls don't do this. That's all right too. We know what we are and I, for one, don't mind it at all." I suddenly realized that I was talking far too much. "I'm sorry. I didn't mean to get carried away. I guess I like you two guys and I want you to like us and I let it bother me that you think of us as prostitutes first and girls second."

"I'm sorry," Brandon said. "I didn't mean to offend you when I said that. I really don't think of you as a prostitute. I like the term 'call girl.' That seems a lot more sophisticated and I really think you two girls are classy. I like you and I sincerely hope I see you again. Please accept my apology."

"Accepted." I looked to see what Lisa and Willard were doing while all this was going on. Lisa was just going down on Willard again. "My god, don't you ever get enough?" I asked her.

After a few minutes, Brandon said, "I don't mean to rush things, but we have to leave for the airport soon, and I'd really like to take a shower again before we leave." Lisa said, "Great idea," and jumped up to head for the shower. Willard and I rose more slowly and followed them. The warm water felt great cascading over my body. I know everyone felt the same because we were all kind of quiet this time, and when we got out, we just got dressed. It was time for Lisa and me to leave.

We were just putting on our coats when the buzzer rang. Willard opened the door and said, "Hello, Dad. Hello, Mr. D." I turned to see the esteemed doctors who had hired our services for the night. They were both prosperous looking gentlemen in their fifties, which makes sense since they were doctors. They said hello to us and shook our hands. This kind of surprised me, but it seems Rachael had told them a little about us, so we didn't seem like two little tarts to them.

Brandon's father turned to him and said, "Well, I hope you boys enjoyed the present we provided you last night."

Brandon was grinning like a little boy. "I can't imagine any better gift for anyone than an evening with these two girls. They are fantastic."

"Perhaps this is an indelicate time, but I'm curious

219

if you thought about Judy a lot last night," said his dad.

"Judy who?" was Brandon's only answer.

Lisa and I said we really had to be going as we laughed at Brandon's answer. Willard's father walked us to the elevator and handed us each a crisp $100 bill. Lisa said, "That's not necessary, Rachael explained to me that the money had been taken care of before we left last night." He said, "That's true, but we decided that if the boys had a good time we would give you each a tip. It looks to us as if they had a wonderful time and you two girls are beautiful. I mean I expected the girls to be attractive, but you two are very pretty. You both look like young college coeds. I'm sure you can use the money."

Lisa again answered, "Thanks. We can use the money. I appreciate the compliments, and we are both college students." Then she glanced down the hall to see if anyone was looking. No one was in the hall so she leaned up to him and kissed his cheek, but when she did this she grabbed his cock and balls and told him to be sure to ask for us for himself and Mr. D. next time he was in town. I couldn't resist smiling at the shock on his face, a shock which shortly turned to a smile and a nod as he turned to go back to the boys' room. Thus ended Lisa's first night at Rachael's. If ever anyone was cut out for this profession, it was definitely Lisa and me, and after that last move on Lisa's part, I would have to say she had the edge.

CHAPTER 23
We Go Back to Rachael's

Lisa and I went downstairs and had the doorman get us a cab. It was an absolutely beautiful day. Lisa looked at me a little strangely when I told the driver to take us to Herald Square. I knew she wanted to go back to Rachael's because we hadn't been paid yet, but I had suddenly remembered our packages in the locker at the subway station. I told her that our twenty-four hours were almost up so we had to either get them or put another quarter in the locker. She had forgotten completely about them in all of our activity during the night. I was a little surprised that I had remembered them myself. Actually, with all we had been through, it was amazing I could remember my own name. Anyway, we went downtown and put another quarter in the locker and then walked over to Lexington Avenue to get something to eat.

I was starving by this time and ordered a great brunch. I had never heard that word when I was growing up in my hometown, but it seems perfect for the meal I usually have on Sunday mornings. While we were eating Lisa asked me if I had thought anymore about the professor. I said that I hadn't, which was true. I really didn't know how to go about getting myself on firmer ground so that he could never use his information against me. "I don't think I want to tell Rachael about him right away," I said. "I think I'll wait until I see Cindy again and see what she has to say about it."

"That's probably a good idea. I wouldn't know what to do if I were in your shoes either. I think you're lucky that he was a horny old goat and wanted to screw you so badly. Suppose he had been a prude and had you kicked out of school. What would you have done?"

"I'm not sure. My first thought was that I would never be able to go home again. My parents would never speak to me for being expelled for prostitution and I wouldn't be able to look anyone in town in the face again. I remember thinking how glad I was that I had over a thousand dollars in the bank. At least I could afford to get an apartment. I would probably continue to work for Rachael. I know I would have gone back to school at some time. But there's no doubt that it would have made my life a lot worse. I'd have survived, but everything would have been worse. I really like my life right now and I don't want to change anything."

"I know what you mean. I'm beginning to like the city more than I did. It's nice to have a little money and be able to afford nice things without worrying about every penny."

When she said that it reminded me of what Cindy had said about saving money. "I hope you don't spend all of the money you make working for Rachael. Cindy told me to save at least half, but I've been saving a lot more than that. When men are buying you dinner as well as paying you for sex, you should definitely save as much as possible."

"That makes a lot of sense. I still have most of the money I earned Wednesday night and Thursday morning. The only money I've spent is what I spent when we were at Macy's yesterday. I guess it would make sense to start putting it in the bank."

As soon as she said "bank," I saw a question on

her face. "What do you do with your money? Doesn't the teller look a little strangely a someone our age depositing so much cash?"

I told her about that exact thing happening to me when I put $500 in the bank one Monday morning. "I know that woman knew how I made the money and I must have turned bright red. I felt like I was there forever, even though it was only a few seconds. So what I do now is I put the money in different branches of my bank in smaller amounts. This is probably stupid, but nobody looks at $150 like they do $500. It's more time-consuming, but I feel a lot more comfortable not having tellers look down their noses at me."

"I think I'll open an account at a bank near you. We seem to spend a lot of time together so we may as well use the same bank."

"I use First National City Bank (later just Citibank), because they have so many branches. I'm sure they would have a branch near Columbia, so you could bank there if you wanted to, or at least you could make a withdrawal easily without coming downtown. They also have blank deposit slips in the bank so you can just fill in your account number. This is real handy because you don't have to remember to bring along a slip all the time. You just have to know your number."

"Sounds good to me," was all Lisa said to end that part of the conversation. We had finished eating and decided it was late enough to go up to Rachael's. Rachael should be up by now and hopefully we could get paid. Then we could come back downtown and pick up our packages and my layaway.

We weren't disappointed. Rachael was pleased with our efforts the previous night. The two doctors were happy that their sons could hardly even think of their girlfriends. It looked like we had accomplished our mission with them. She gave Lisa a lot of praise for her work before leaving with Willard and Brandon. "A new girl is always an unknown quantity to me before a night like last night. I never really know if she can handle the pressure until she is put to the test. Sharon had proven her worth to me her first Saturday night here, and you did the same last night. I am very pleased to have both of you working for me."

She reached in her desk drawer for two envelopes. "Sharon, I want you to know that Lisa made more money than you did last night because she had five men while you only had three before you left for the Plaza."

I looked at Lisa with true admiration. "Five. My god, when did you find the time? I saw one of the men leave your room. He looked like he could hardly walk, so I know you weren't rushing them."

Rachael and I both cracked up at Lisa's response to this. "When I fuck 'em, they stay fucked." I knew I was going to like working with her for a long time.

Rachael then asked us about working the next weekend, but we couldn't because Thursday was Thanksgiving and we both planned to go home. Rachael said she had assumed this would be the case, but that would be all right, because she was normally not busy on the holidays. As we were leaving, she asked us how we were getting home. I said I was taking the bus, because it was the cheapest way and my parents wouldn't understand how I could afford to fly. I don't know why I was surprised when Lisa said she was too. I guess I had assumed she would fly, but then it occurred to me that I didn't know where she lived. I was shocked when she said she lived in a city about fifty miles closer to New York than I did. We were going to ride the same bus home. Sometimes the world is a real small place. When we finally left the house, we were discussing meeting Wednesday night at the Port Authority where we were to catch the bus.

We caught a cab back downtown and spent the rest of the day window shopping before Lisa went back to Columbia. We both had some more studying to do and I had to talk to Cindy yet about my problem with Mr. Kenningston, but everything seemed fine right now. I was looking forward to Thanksgiving. Not only would I get a chance to see Bill, but I might even see Lisa. I would definitely see her over Christmas vacation. Life was looking great.

CHAPTER 24
My Problem with Mr. Kenningston Is Solved

After stopping for my package in the locker, we went shopping at Macy's before going back to my dorm about 4:00 that afternoon. I was surprised that Cindy was already back and studying hard. She is naturally smart so she learns very easily. I almost never see her concentrating so hard.

I was just as surprised at Lisa's greeting to Cindy. She waltzed over to her and gave her a big, as in huge, kiss right on the lips. "I just wanted to thank you for introducing Sharon and me to Rachael. I feel like a million bucks."

Cindy was immediately interested in us. Totally ignoring the book in front of her, she asked, "Well, what did you two little sluts do this weekend that brought this on?"

I was still silent as Lisa jumped in and said, "Oh, we just fucked our asses off... and loved every minute of it. At least I did and I'm pretty sure that Sharon has no complaints."

"Oh no, I have to admit I loved Saturday night and this morning. Just when I began to feel tired and was looking forward to only having a couple of more customers, we were taken out for dinner and spent the night in the Plaza with a couple of doctors' sons. I think we changed their whole philosophy. They were much too serious before."

I was surprised and a little angry when Lisa brought up my incident with Mr. Kenningston. I wasn't really ready to deal with this yet, but my anger passed as Cindy seemed genuinely concerned and a little alarmed. "Sharon, he can get you in a lot of trouble. But I know a couple of guys who can scare the hell out of him . . ."

"I don't want him to get hurt. I never want anyone to get hurt because of what I'm doing with you and Rachael . . ."

"You didn't let me finish. I was going to add that Rachael probably knows someone who can apply pressure without any threat of violence. We should tell her right away."

I was a little reluctant to bring Rachael into what I considered my personal problems, but Cindy insisted. She went out and called Rachael who must have said to come up and see her right away, because the three of us were shortly in a cab back to the Upper East Side.

When we got to Rachael's, Maria ushered us in to the study immediately. Rachael was very concerned about this whole thing. She asked me why I hadn't mentioned anything about this when I saw her earlier, and I truthfully told her that I hadn't wanted to involve her in something I considered to be my problem. She seemed genuinely shocked by this attitude. "Sharon, I don't ever want you to think that your problems don't concern me. After all, if you weren't working here you wouldn't be having this problem. If I couldn't help you, I would have no reason to keep half of the money you earn here."

"I guess that's true enough. I hadn't really thought of it that way. It seems fair to me that you take half for letting us work here and supplying us with customers, but to get back to Mr. Kenningston, I wouldn't want anything to happen to him. I mean anything serious like an injury or something. I don't know why I feel this way, but I do. It is very important to me that nothing happen to him. I really couldn't live with myself if he were injured because of me."

"Honey, no one is going to injure him, but for the life of me, I can't see why you are so concerned about him. You can believe me when I tell you that everyone, absolutely everyone, has something that he wants kept quiet. We'll just find out what his secret is and then let him know that we know. He won't be able to threaten you again."

I answered, "Anyone in our business has to believe

that everyone has secrets. I like your solution to this. To tell you the truth, last night I was having such a good time that I only thought of it once, when Lisa and I were at the Plaza. The two boys we were with said you could probably help me, but when Lisa and I came up here earlier today I really didn't think of it. I was in such a good mood that the whole situation never entered my mind."

"Well, I'm glad you finally came to your senses and decided to let me help you. I'll have a detective I know get on it right away. By the time you leave for your Thanksgiving vacation, Mr. Kenningston will have apologized to you for making a terrible mistake."

I had to smile at her diplomatic way of expressing his apology. I was of course guilty. He would actually be apologizing for taking advantage of me and threatening me with expulsion, but I liked her phrasing better. "It will be nice to have the whole matter resolved by the time I leave for vacation. I sure would hate to have my parents get a letter from the school while I was home."

We all left shortly after that and went back to the dorm. Cindy and Lisa both tried to reassure me that everything was going to be fine. I appreciated Lisa trying to help, but it was Cindy's assurances that rated higher with me because she had known Rachael longer.

When I got a phone call from Mr. Kenningston Tuesday morning, I made an appointment to see him right after my last class. Unfortunately, my classes ran late that day and it was 5:00 p.m. when I finally got to his office. The entire school was almost

228

empty because most of the students were leaving early for vacation. It was beginning to look like I might be alone in some classes the next morning. I purposely wore the same outfit I had worn Friday night when I had my previous meeting with him, but I was putting on a bravura act that I didn't really feel. I was very nervous when he ushered me into his office and asked me to sit down. After all, I wasn't sure Rachael could really take care of this so easily. It was entirely possible that he would only get angry at my attempt to protect myself. I could be a lot worse off than I was on Sunday. When he sat at his desk, the chair was facing off to the side so he was looking out the window when he sat down. It made me very uneasy when he just sat there for awhile without saying anything. Finally he seemed to remember that I was there: "Sharon:"

"Yes."

"I'm sure you remember our last appointment and what took place."

"Yes." I remembered what Brandon and Willard had said about taping my next appointment with him. It had occurred to me that he might be taping this entire conversation so I was being very careful of what I said. I suddenly decided to see if I could get him to go elsewhere for the rest of the interview. "Look, can we go somewhere else to talk. I feel very claustrophobic in here." He looked straight at me when I said this, but he nodded his head in agreement and we both got up to leave. When he agreed to leave his office, I knew I was all right. I just knew he wouldn't come down hard on me anywhere else. The hallways were totally deserted as we walked toward the elevator, but I didn't feel the least bit nervous anymore.

We walked a few minutes in silence as I waited for him to start talking. "I had a call from the mortgage officer at my bank yesterday afternoon. It seems that I have offended some powerful people. It is my understanding that if I don't make an apology to you and put your mind at ease, my mortgage may be called in thirty days. Needless to say I don't have enough cash to pay it off. I had no idea that you had such powerful friends, but you definitely have my apology for my error in accusing you of any wrongdoing. I'm definitely sorry this entire thing happened." He looked really despondent as we continued to walk in the hall. (We had long since passed the elevator.) "However, I do want you to know that I would never have made any trouble for you after Friday night. My word was good. I'm a little surprised that I was so easily seduced, but I would never have gone back on my word."

Needless to say I was feeling pretty good by now. I don't really know what got into me, but when we walked by a Men's Room sign I had a sudden impulse to show him there were no hard feelings. I grabbed his hand and led him inside. The look on his face was absolute astonishment and total bewilderment. "I'm sorry about our misunderstanding too, but I'm not sorry about everything that happened."

"What are you doing?"

"I'm going to show you that there are no hard feelings on my part," and I led him to one of the stalls and pushed him inside. He stopped talking when my hands undid his belt and zipper. I had his pants down and pushed him back on the seat before he could think of any response. His cock was standing straight up as I pulled my skirt above my waist giving him a quick glimpse of my pantiless pussy before I straddled him and sat down on his cock in one stroke. God, this felt good. It almost always felt good, but being in a Men's Room was a new experience for me and this felt deliciously naughty. I grabbed his head and kissed him real hard as he began to buck upward as we continued fucking. My cunt was squeezing his prick with every muscle it had when he flooded me with his cum. His tongue was deep in my mouth teasing my own tongue while my cunt was gripping his cock as he continued to pump his cum into me. When he finally stopped coming we both relaxed a little and caught our breath.

He had an extremely puzzled look on his face as I remained sitting on top of him with his cock still in my pussy. "Why did you do this?"

"I told you I wanted you to know there are no hard feelings. This is the best way I know of to convince you that I am sincere. As far as I am concerned the incident is closed."

"Obviously, I'm relieved that everything is all right again, but in a way I'm going to regret not having an excuse to have you in my office. You really are very good. I can see why men pay for your favors. I . . ."

He stopped talking as we heard the door open. I immediately put my legs up higher so they couldn't be seen from outside the stall while he held me so I wouldn't tip backwards. We were deathly still as the other man urinated just a few feet from us. I don't know why but my feelings of fear began to retreat and I had to put a hand over my mouth to prevent a serious case of the giggles. I know this sounds really stupid, because we both would have been in a lot of trouble if the wrong person caught us in here. Anyway, the problem went away with our visitor. Strangely enough, Mr. Kenningston's erection had not gone away. He was as hard as a brick and ready for another round. I raised my eyebrows in surprise and lowered my legs as he started to fuck me. He stood up still holding me so I couldn't fall backward. Then he leaned me against the wall of the stall and simply fucked the hell out of me. My legs were wrapped tightly around him when he rammed me hard against the wall and came in me. God, I loved that feeling. I don't know why I loved it so much. I was trying to be cute by showing him that there were no hard feelings and he was the one giving me the great fuck. I was kind of pleased that I didn't cum, though. It was probably the fear I still felt (giggles or no giggles), but it did leave me with a little respect. He could fuck me really good, but he wasn't able to fuck me to orgasm.

After he finished coming the second time he was done for the night. Either that, or his fear of being caught was becoming more powerful, because he was definitely in a hurry to get dressed and out of here before anyone else should happen along. He went to the door and told me the coast was clear so we both escaped with our reputations intact. (Ha. Ha.) As we rode the elevator to the ground floor, he turned and said, "Well, Sharon, this meeting has certainly turned out differently than I imagined it would."

"I've got to agree with that. I had no idea this was going to happen, but I had a good time in there." As we were stopping I suddenly stood up on my toes and gave him a quick kiss on the cheek saying, "I'll see you when I get back from vacation," and stepped out of the elevator and left the building. I wondered all weekend what he would think of that statement. I wasn't sure I knew myself.

A selection of Erotica
from Headline

EROTICA

BARE NECESSITIES	Anonymous	£3.99 □
BEDROOM EYES	Anonymous	£3.99 □
CARNAL DAYS	Anonymous	£4.50 □
ECSTASY ITALIAN STYLE	Anonymous	£3.99 □
EROS IN SOCIETY	Anonymous	£3.99 □
EROS ON THE GRAND TOUR	Anonymous	£2.99 □
EROTICON DREAMS	Anonymous	£4.99 □
INTIMATE POSITIONS	Anonymous	£4.50 □
LOVE BITES	Anonymous	£4.50 □
SWEET SENSATIONS	Anonymous	£4.50 □
THE COMPLETE EVELINE	Anonymous	£4.99 □
THE PLEASURES OF WOMEN	Anonymous	£3.99 □
THE SECRET DIARY OF MATA HARI	Anonymous	£3.50 □
THE STORY OF HONEY O	Anonymous	£3.99 □
A VICTORIAN LOVER OF WOMEN	Faye Rossignol	£3.50 □
THE FFRENCH HOUSE	Faye Rossignol	£3.99 □
SWEET FANNY	Faye Rossignol (Ed)	£2.99 □
THE TEMPTATIONS OF CREMORNE	Anonymous	£3.99 □
VENUS IN PARIS	Anonymous	£3.99 □

All Headline books are available at your local bookshop or newsagent, or can be ordered direct from the publisher. Just tick the titles you want and fill in the form below. Prices and availability subject to change without notice.

Headline Book Publishing PLC, Cash Sales Department, PO Box 11, Falmouth, Cornwall, TR10 9EN, England.

Please enclose a cheque or postal order to the value of the cover price and allow the following for postage and packing:
UK & BFPO: £1.00 for the first book, 50p for the second book and 30p for each additional book ordered up to a maximum charge of £3.00.
OVERSEAS & EIRE: £2.00 for the first book, £1.00 for the second book and 50p for each additional book.

Name ....

Address ....

....

....